Cressida: No Mystery

Marie Belloc Lowndes

Originally published 1928
W. Heinemann, London, U.K.

This edition published 2023 by

The Oleander Press
16 Orchard Street
Cambridge
CB1 1JT

www.oleanderpress.com

ISBN: 9781915475329

Sign up to our infrequent newsletter
to **receive a free ePub** of
Fatality in Fleet Street
by Christopher St John Sprigg and get
news of new titles, discounts and give-aways!

www.oleanderpress.com/golden-age-crime

A CIP catalogue record for the book
is available from the British Library.

Cover design, typesetting & ebook: neorelix

Cressida: No Mystery

"I have this night digged up a mandrake."
"Say you ?"
"And I am grown mad with it."

The Duchess of Malfi

1

EVEN THE TYPE OF Englishman to whom life has taught the supreme value of silence sometimes feels, and yields to, a sudden impulse to utter his thoughts. So, "Alice? Take care!" whispered Colonel Slade, smiling into the animated face of his widowed hostess. "You look almost indecently pleased."

"I'm much more than pleased; I'm mad with joy, George! No early-Victorian mamma ever felt happier at her demure chick catching a virtuous duke than I feel now. Just look at the child! She's absolutely transformed. And such an improvement in her looks, too. Larry gave her that lovely old embroidered shawl this morning, and it really suits her."

The country luncheon party was made up of Lady Bignor; her faithful friend and indulgent critic, George Slade; Mr. and Mrs. Lancaster, the elderly rector of the parish and his worn-looking wife; Dr. McLeod, confidant and medical adviser of the prosperous Surrey countryside; and last, though by no means least, either in their own estimation, or in that of the other five persons there, Lady Bignor's niece, Lizzie Bowden, and Lizzie's fiancé, Captain Wortle. It was to celebrate their engagement that these old and tried friends had been brought together today.

Though it was now December the eighteenth, and so just a week from Christmas, the dining room of Millhanger House was airy, deliciously warm, and full of light and colour. Lady Bignor loved beauty, and could afford to indulge her love. She had built her house at the apex of a high hill; each room commanded a noble view, and bore the imprint of her bold and unusual taste.

The walls of the dining room were tinted sealing-wax red, and on the narrow black marble dining table gleamed a service of old lapis lazuli Venetian glass.

Colonel Slade had made no reply to Lady Bignor's triumphant answer to his warning remark. For one thing her words somewhat jarred on him. During the four war years he had been in France, he had rubbed up his French; and now he reminded himself of the proverb, "*Toute verité n'est pas bonne à dire.*"

Even so, after a while, he put on his eyeglasses, and allowed his shrewd, if kindly, glance to travel down the shining marble table till they rested on the two, the girl and the young man, who were now sitting side by side, exactly opposite Lady Bignor and himself.

And then, with that cruel candour which even the best-natured man, if intelligent, uses in the inner chamber of his mind, he told himself that, transformed or not, Lizzie Bowden was still damned plain, poor child.

For one thing, Lizzie was fat – unnaturally so, for a girl of twenty-one. For another, with her pale face, pale lips, pale eyes, and pale red hair, the bride-elect appeared, to him at least, a grotesque caricature of the aunt who had been lovely in her day. Twenty-five years ago Lady Bignor had had masses of brilliant auburn hair allied to a beautiful complexion; and she was still, even now, a very attractive-looking woman.

Colonel Slade, a friend from Harrow days of Lizzie Bowden's now long-dead father, had become joint trustee and guardian, with Lady Bignor, to the girl's large fortune. This was why he both knew and, in a sense, liked Lizzie better than did most of the people who were brought into contact with her.

He had come to be aware, sometimes uncomfortably so, that in a heavy old-fashioned way she was clever, and not lacking in character. Though she had only come of age a few weeks ago, she had already shown herself both intelligent and understanding with regard to what were now her investments.

But – well, there were a number of "buts," concerning Lizzie's nature and character, of which her ex-guardian was ruefully conscious. The able family solicitor who had charge of Miss Bowden's legal interests had observed, the other day, what a pity it was that his young client was so limited and so obstinate, not to say stupid, in her outlook on life. He, George Slade, had combated that view, and given it as his opinion that the future Mrs. Larry Wortle, in spite of her lack of looks and ungainly ways, was a young woman to be reckoned with.

And now, while gazing with a certain painful interest at the two, Colonel Slade wondered whether the young man who was soon to be her husband realised that in certain circumstances Lizzie might be something of a handful?

With a touch of concern and regret he told himself that it was a real pity, in her own interest, that the girl took so little trouble, not only with regard to her appearance, but with regard to her manner. Even when evidently trying to be pleasant, she would often be brusque and dogmatic to a most irritating degree. But then good temper had never been, so her critic reminded himself, Lizzie Bowden's strong suit.

He had once surprised her in a fit of violent rage against a maid who had spoilt a muslin frock by putting too hot an iron on it, and though the incident had taken place a good many years ago, he had never forgotten it.

It came back to him, today, with disagreeable vividness.

He had spoken to her that day very seriously as to the folly, as well as to the unseemliness, of such lack of self-control. But though she had listened to what he had said with apparent submission and respect, he had been well aware that his severe, if measured, words of rebuke and warning had not reached her mind. She had thought, and went on thinking, her outburst against the careless maid justified.

But George Slade had a magnanimous nature, and at last, with a slight feeling of shame at his over-candid thoughts and memories, he told himself that bygones must now be bygones. Without going so far as his dear, impulsive Alice Bignor had gone, when declaring her niece to be transformed, he could not but see that the fact of her engagement had brought about a great change. Lizzie did look far happier, and even better-looking, than usual today, and that though she had a cold.

And then, hardly aware that he was doing so, Colonel Slade fixed his attention on Lizzie Bowden's fiancé; and his kindly face stiffened, and became hard.

Tall, dark, well-groomed (hateful phrase), entirely idle and pleasure-loving, sufficiently good at games and sport to be always sure of a welcome in a certain kind of country house, in the halcyon days "before the war" Larry Wortle would have drifted into the only existence nature had made him fit to lead. The small income left him by a father who had not been over-fortunate in business would then have sufficed, not only to keep him in good clothes, and provide the petty cash required for tips and railway fares, but to have paid, also, the rent of a furnished room within hail of the good club which had early become one of his most valuable assets in life.

Larry Wortle had joined up at once in August 1914; and hadn't done at all badly. Of that creditable fact his present critic quickly reminded himself. But, after the war, the young man had drifted into an extravagant, mad-for-pleasure set. There he had been persuaded to put the whole of his small capital in a business gamble which promised large returns; and in a few months he had lost everything. Then had followed various jobs of the commission-basis type, on which he had starved rather than lived. At the time, some two months ago, when he had first met and set careful, deliberate, siege to Lizzie Bowden, he would have been quite "down and out," but for the kindness of an uncle who grudgingly kept him going, while trying, unsuccessfully, to find him some form of steady salaried work.

Now, with his fortunes marvellously retrieved, Larry Wortle sat by his stolid-looking heiress – wearing a suit cut by a better tailor than he, George Slade, could afford to patronise in these hard times – sipping with the air of a connoisseur, a glass of Lady Bignor's 1906 champagne.

And yet, even so, the unspoken words rose to the older man's lips, "I wouldn't have taken on Lizzie for a million a year, when I was a young chap!"

But he choked back the unkind thought, and turned, with a feeling of relief, to the dear friend on his left – his delightful, easy-going, sunny- tempered hostess. Though he might privately deplore her frank satisfaction in Lizzie's engagement, Colonel Slade could not but rejoice at what was, after all, a bit of rare good fortune for Lizzie's aunt.

Small wonder that Lady Bignor looked almost indecently pleased that the sullen-natured, self-willed niece, to whom she had been so truly kind, if not in any sense motherly, for over ten long years, had chosen her own path at last, and that path, matrimony.

"George?"

He turned to her quickly.

"A penny for your thoughts!"

He evaded the gay challenge by a serious question. "Is Lizzie's wedding day fixed?"

"As there's nothing to wait for, I've suggested the third or fourth of February. They'll spend ten days at Rotherham Castle, and then they'll go to Egypt, taking with them the car she's giving him as a wedding present."

"It sounds very grand—"

Lady Bignor's eyes twinkled in answer to her old friend's dry comment. "Larry has already engaged a valet-chauffeur. That young man likes to have everything handsome about him, George; he's quite unlike our little Lizzie there."

As Colonel Slade made no answer to that undoubtedly true observation, she exclaimed, in a very different tone, "Isn't it wonderful to know, my dear, I am going to be free at last?"

The man she had just called her "dear" reddened deeply under his tan, and, seeing that, Lady Bignor felt queerly touched. Long, silent fidelity has something very pleasant about it to any woman, and this woman had a warm, affectionate nature.

"What are your plans?" he asked quietly. "I take it, Alice, that you mean to make good use of your freedom?"

She hesitated, just a little ashamed of herself, as she met the steady gaze of his faithful eyes.

Though he apparently didn't know it – "men are so stupid about that sort of thing" – she of course meant to marry her kind devoted George some day; and very, very happy she intended to make him. But she felt she was entitled to a last fling, so, "Dear, delightful Monte Carlo for me," she answered lightly. "At any rate, till Easter."

"Are you going alone?"

There was that in his quick look at her, a wistful, longing, even ardent, look, that made her heart beat a little faster than usual. But how silly, how mad, of this dear foolish man to suppose, as she feared he did suppose, that he would like Monte Carlo, even in her company? If they were there together, he would loathe it, and that would make her miserable.

"Alone? Oh no, George, I hate being alone. I'm thinking of asking Cressida Daryl to go with me as my guest."

She waited a moment. Her heart was still beating. At least she supposed it was her heart? Rather absurd at her age! All the same, why didn't George Slade see that now was his chance? Why didn't he grip her hand under the table, and – and—

But George Slade did nothing of the kind. He only looked at her again, in that dumb, queer, hungry way that had moved her so, just now.

So she went on, a little breathlessly, "It's great fun travelling with Cressida. Wherever she goes, she either finds a host of amusing friends, not to speak of lovers, or else she makes new ones! I asked her to spend Christmas here, before all this affair was settled," she nodded towards the engaged couple. "But she was, naturally enough, already booked – and by that French duchess who's taken a big place in Leicestershire. She told me, poor girl, that she'd hardly enough money to pay her fare there and back, to say nothing of tips – her bank having shut off supplies. As I had a bit of luck the other day over an old investment, I sent her fifty pounds."

"You are too kind, Alice," he said in a low voice.

What an old fool he had been to suppose, even for a moment, that—?

"Indeed I'm not," she exclaimed. "Cressida's more like a child of my own than that girl over there has ever been. And when she likes she can be – oh, such good company!"

"I know Miss Daryl is regarded as a very attractive creature," he observed meditatively. "But lately she's been overdoing the pace. She seems very delicate, and as for looks – well, far too thin, for my old-fashioned taste."

George Slade's hostess felt a touch of tenderness, of secret gratitude, sweep over her. Even as a girl she had had what in those days was delicately called "a figure"; and now, alas, she had to be very careful. She had only eaten, of the excellent luncheon all those round her had enjoyed, a small slice of pheasant.

"Then you've seen Cressida lately?" she asked.

"I was with her at that big shoot about a month ago; and she lost over ten pounds at bridge one afternoon. I don't know that I'd take her to Monte Carlo, Alice, if I were you."

"I shall give her a hundred francs a day to play with. Her company will be worth far more than that to me."

He lowered his voice. "I wish for her sake that Lizzie Bowden knew how to spend her money as cleverly and kindly as you spend yours."

"The child's not mean," said Lady Bignor quickly. "But in a sense you're right, George. If only Lizzie had been left my lovely

Cressida's little income to manage, and if Cressida had Lizzie's big fortune to spend – how happy each of them would be!"

"You would have had Lizzie tied to you for the rest of your life," he said shortly.

"Why, yes, I suppose I should. Still, I do think that Larry Wortle likes her, George?"

There was a note of appeal in her low voice, and he felt as if she was "willing him" to give a reassuring answer.

But George Slade was an honest – sometimes Alice Bignor told herself a tiresomely honest, man. So, "Do you?" he said drily.

She made a restless movement, as she answered defensively, "I've known men devoted to such hideous women. And, what's queerer still, often they were other men's wives."

"So have I," he agreed. And then, remembering one special case of the kind, he gave a quick, rather shamed, chuckle.

"I think Larry's already a little afraid of Lizzie," Lady Bignor observed, speaking her thoughts aloud.

"I'm glad of that," he said grimly. "I don't think she'd stand much nonsense. I can imagine Lizzie most unpleasantly jealous."

Lizzie's aunt smiled, a roguish little smile. "It would take her a long time to find out anything to be jealous about. She has such an uncommonly good opinion of herself, poor child."

"I wouldn't advise Lizzie's husband to count too much on that."

Lady Bignor looked down the table, and saw with satisfaction that her niece was laughing happily at something her fiancé had just whispered to her.

"I think that young man is very well aware on which side his bread is buttered," she said decidedly.

But in return Colonel Slade only muttered, "I wonder," while inwardly was telling himself that Larry Wortle didn't look the sort of chap who can stand corn.

Lady Bignor glanced round the table. "Everyone's finished now, so I wish you'd get up and say something pretty, George. After all, this is a kind of betrothal party, you know."

He rose obediently, and the murmur of talk died away, as, holding up his glass of champagne, he began, in a tone of mock solemnity:

"Ladies and gentlemen! I ask you to drink to the health and happiness of a very fortunate man, Larrymore Wortle, and to that of our young friend, Elizabeth Bowden, known to us all as 'Lizzie,' soon to be joined in the bonds of holy matrimony. May they live to celebrate their golden wedding day, and, for the matter of that, their diamond wedding day."

Everyone there, except the two whose health was about to be drunk, rose to their feet. Glasses clinked. "Elizabeth Bowden—" "Captain Wortle—" "Larry!" "Lizzie!"

The head parlourmaid, whose apparently effortless efficiency roused envy in the heart of Mrs. Lancaster, the clergyman's wife, whose housework, when not done by herself, was done by a village girl aged fourteen – laid a sheet of paper headed "Telephone," in front of her mistress.

"Miss Daryl is holding the line, my lady."

"What luck!" cried Lady Bignor delightedly. "Cressida Daryl offers herself for Christmas. The people to whom she was going today have chucked her. She says a man she knows can motor her down here this afternoon."

She looked up at the parlourmaid. "Say I shall be delighted to see Miss Daryl today; and that I hope she'll stay till after the New Year."

Larry Wortle, at the other end of the table, turned to his fiancée. "Is that the Miss Daryl?" he asked with a touch of eagerness.

Lizzie Bowden felt a little surprised, and not over-pleased at the way the question was put. "Well, yes, I suppose Cressida is the Miss Daryl," she answered grudgingly.

"I've heard such a lot about her, and I've always wanted to meet her!" he exclaimed.

Lizzie stared at him with genuine surprise.

"I don't think you'll like her at all, Larry. In fact, I know you won't. She's a fearful self-advertiser, always in the picture-papers – and she simply lives at nightclubs and those sort of places. Of course she can't afford it, for she's very poor. But she doesn't mind being in debt – not one bit."

Wortle felt a sudden flash of sympathy with the Miss Daryl. But he told himself, quickly, that as Lizzie evidently didn't like her, he must mind his step.

All the same Lizzie couldn't prevent his feeling secretly overjoyed at the thought that Cressida Daryl was to form part of what he had supposed would be an extremely dull Christmas house party.

Lady Bignor's coming guest was not only what very old ladies and gentlemen still call "a beauty"; she was an amusing, sometimes a brilliant, talker; noted, also, as an amateur actress; and one of the few girls who formed part of the smart young married women set. Again and again Larry Wortle had been on the point of meeting Cressida Daryl. But the London world in which she moved and had her agreeable, popular, being, was a great cut above the world he had frequented in the jovial days which had preceded his "crash."

True, he hovered on the fringe of that high little world, and he fully intended to form part of it as soon as Lizzie's golden key to the only kind of life he loved, and of which he had learnt the shibboleths, had passed into his keeping.

Lady Bignor had been right in her half-suspicion that the young man was already a little afraid of his future wife. Though he had reason to think himself clever in the management of women, Lizzie Bowden often surprised him. And now, not for the first time, he told himself, with a feeling of discomfort, that there was a touch of censoriousness in her attitude to her fellows which sat oddly, as well as disagreeably, on one of her age and upbringing.

However, deep in his heart, Larry Wortle was well aware that in her queer, secretive way, Lizzie already loved him passionately.

He had had a remarkable proof of that fact in London this morning, before coming down to Millhanger House. The lawyers engaged in drawing up the marriage settlement had informed him that, on Miss Bowden's instructions, a thousand a year was going to be settled on him, Captain Wortle, on his wedding day. Further, that the generous young lady had arranged for two hundred and fifty pounds to be paid into his banking account this very day, December the eighteenth, as, ahem! a Christmas gift.

Lizzie's present was a real godsend, and all the more welcome because so utterly unexpected. He had been horribly, he told himself degradingly, hard up, till this happy morning. Indeed, he hadn't known how he would get through the weeks before his marriage day! Thanks to Lizzie, and her thoughtful generosity, all was now, as he joyously put it to himself, quite O.K.

Small wonder that he had bought for her, on his way to the station, a really beautiful old embroidered yellow shawl. Larry had a pretty taste in such things, and he secretly deplored his fiancée's curious lack of knowledge of what was becoming to herself.

After the train had left Victoria, as he sat back in a corner seat of the well-warmed, comfortable, first-class compartment – no longer, now, did he have to travel third class – he had gazed with exultant eyes at the announcement of his engagement in *The Times*.

Then had followed on the one hand a kind, on the other an obviously ecstatic, welcome, to this agreeable, admirably "run" house. Small wonder that Larry Wortle looked and felt happy, as well as prosperous, today.

Lizzie had made her cold an excuse to wear her lover's latest gift at lunch, and he told himself, now, that she certainly looked far nicer today than she was wont to do, when clad in the type of sports jumper and skimpy skirt which is so trying to the fat and plain.

Larry Wortle, who had not yet had an opportunity of thanking his fiancée in private for her welcome Christmas gift, told himself another thing just before they both rose from table. Till today he had thought his future wife far too careful about money, even ridiculously so, for so rich a girl. But now he believed that if mean to others, and even to herself, she would ever be generous to the only human being who, as even he had come to realise, really counted in her life, namely his fortunate self.

2

AFTER LUNCH, COFFEE WAS always served in the drawing room, so the whole party went across the large square hall round which had been built Millhanger House.

Lady Bignor's drawing room was a charming room, and also what some charming rooms are not, extremely liveable in. The buttercup-yellow walls made an admirable background for a pair of old Chinese white lacquer cabinets. And the wide low sofas and deep easy chairs, upholstered in cream-coloured horsehair, and heaped up with turquoise-blue cushions, were exceedingly comfortable.

The general colouring and furnishings of the apartment were far kinder to the mistress of Millhanger House than to her niece; but, even so, Lizzie showed to more advantage here than in the dining room.

"The child looks really happy at last," murmured Mrs. Lancaster, addressing Dr. McLeod.

"That's because Miss Lizzie knows that she is going to wear the breeches," he whispered back.

"D'you really think she will?"

"I do! Lizzie has a good bit more to her than any of you think for, Mrs. Lancaster; and, to my thinking, yon young man won't have quite as easy a time as he expects."

"She's very fond of him," said the lady defensively. "I watched her during lunch. She had only eyes and ears for Captain Wortle."

"That won't last," he said drily.

"It does sometimes. Think of Mrs. McLeod?"

His face softened. "Present company is always excepted! But I must stop gossiping now. May I give you and the rector a lift?"

Colonel Slade was staying on till after Christmas; and after Dr. McLeod and the rector and Mrs. Lancaster had gone, their hostess turned to the three that remained.

"Now then," she exclaimed, "what are we all going to do with ourselves this afternoon? Would you care to drive into Dorking with me, George? As for Lizzie and Larry – they, I hope, can be trusted to look after themselves."

Addressing the girl who was now standing by her lover's side, she went on, in a kindly tone, "I've ordered a fire to be lit in the study every morning, so that you two can be there as much as you like, answering letters of congratulation, and so on. Still, before you settle down there this afternoon, I suggest, Larry, that you take Lizzie out for a good walk. She doesn't take half enough exercise—" She nearly added, "she'd look very different if she did."

"Aunt Alice – you've forgotten that I have a cold?"

It was the old, pre-engagement, Lizzie, who spoke in that cross, self-important tone.

Lady Bignor turned away with an impatient movement. How pleasant to know that Cressida Daryl would soon be here. Cressida who was so amusing, so agreeable, and so good-tempered, as well as so good to look upon!

As Lizzie Bowden was a young woman who always knew her own mind, a very few minutes after her aunt and Colonel Slade had left the house she was established in the book-lined study, sitting on her lover's knee, and listening with a sensation of intense, almost painful, joy, to his muttered terms of endearment.

Although she could have married, as the saying is, three or four times since she had "come out," at a large, dull ball, given for her in Belgrave Square by a kind godmother, Larry Wortle was the first man who had ever made love to her. And, while well aware that he was attractive to women, he had been surprised at the girl's passionate response to his tepid, if earnest, wooing.

But today Larry did feel that gratitude which, in some masculine natures, is akin to love.

Suddenly drawing her closer to him, he whispered, "You are a brick, darling! When Mr. Coxe told me this morning about that splendid Christmas present of yours – well, you could have knocked me down with a small feather."

She was a little puzzled, as well as much moved, by the thrill of authentic emotion that had come into his low, vibrant voice.

Lizzie had far too good an opinion of herself to suspect, even dimly, that the endearing phrases Larry Wortle had already uttered came from the head, and not from the heart, of her lover.

She jumped off his knee, and stood looking down, her plain face all aglow with feeling, into his fine, long-lashed eyes.

"That's nothing!" she exclaimed, breathing a little quickly. "I hated the thought of your not being—" She did not quite know what word to use, till at last she found the inadequate, yet to her expressive, word, "comfortable."

He moved a little forward in the deep easy chair which had held the two of them. Putting out his hand, he tried to pull her down on to his knee again.

But Lizzie had not yet had her say out; and, after a few moments, she exclaimed, "That horrid uncle of yours didn't pay up all your debts, did he?"

"He has now," acknowledged the young man grudgingly. "But he's not on the generous side. In fact, he's frightfully near. So your present, darling, was a good deal more than welcome—"

And then, just as he was feeling, as he put it to himself, really affectionate for once to this odd girl who was so soon to be his wife, she said something which irritated him keenly.

Drawing up a little chair, she sat down, heavily, upon it. "I can't make out," she said slowly, "how you came to be in debt at all, Larry?"

He felt sharply annoyed, indeed more than annoyed, angered, by the half-question. He had been compelled to "make a clean breast of it" with regard to his financial troubles past and present, to Colonel Slade, before the engagement had been formally sanctioned. So he told himself that Lizzie must surely know all about his unlucky investment, and so on. It was easy for her to talk – unnaturally averse as she seemed to be from any form of extravagance, and born, too, with a silver spoon in her mouth.

"I suppose I got into foolish ways during the war. When one thought every minute was going to be one's last – well, it made one feel like 'going it' when one had the luck to be home on leave," he said sorely.

"But that was such a long time ago – the war, I mean."

He looked at her earnest, obstinate, uncomprehending, face, with a feeling of repulsion.

"It sometimes seems like a hundred years ago, and sometimes as if it were only yesterday!" he exclaimed.

"I can't think what you mean, Larry."

The commonplace words were uttered in a cold, disagreeable tone. And Larry Wortle realised, with a sensation of something like fear, that a part of the peculiar, secretive, sensitive human entity known to her little world of unimaginative people as "dull tiresome Lizzie Bowden," in a sense saw through him, while yet so much of her was blind.

Allow her to burrow into his comparatively innocent, if extravagant, past? Fiercely he answered his own question, "Not much!"

Then all at once he saw her face soften. Perhaps his silence made her realise, at long last, that she had angered him? Be that as it may, Larry Wortle, seeing that change in her expression, reminded himself that to bring his future wife to heel was only a question of taking a little trouble.

With a sudden movement which took her by surprise, he leant forward and, roughly drawing her on to his knee again, "Don't let's waste time in talking of horrible, hateful things that won't ever happen again," he whispered, "when we can kiss, kiss, kiss!"

And as she lay in his arms, inarticulate, while yet trembling with tense emotion, there came over him a sensation – that of cruel triumph – he had not experienced with any other woman. And with that sensation of cruel triumph was coupled a strain of contemptuous amusement at her simplicity in accepting, with such pathetic delight, false coin for true.

There are moments in most human lives which become retrospectively memorable. Such a moment is etched deep on the tablets of more than one mind concerning what, at the time, seemed such a trivial incident – the first meeting between Cressida Daryl and Larry Wortle.

That immortal moment occurred late in the afternoon which followed Lizzie Bowden's betrothal luncheon.

At Wortle's suggestion, he and his fiancée, in spite of her cold, had at last gone out for a short walk up and down the only level path in the steep grounds of Millhanger House. And they had just come in, and were waiting for tea to be brought into the drawing room, when they heard the sounds of a motor sweeping up the incline which led to the stone-paved forecourt of the house.

"That's not our car," exclaimed Lizzie. And as they both ran out to see who it could be, "It must be Cressida! How stupid of me to forget that she was arriving today—"

The front door was flung open and, together with a blast of cold air, Cressida Daryl, her tall, slender, almost attenuated figure wrapped in a splendid mink fur coat, and wearing on her pale golden hair a red leather cap, glided into the hall.

Under that superb coat, the gift of a kind man friend, Cressida wore a red leather jumper matching her cap. The short skirt under the jumper was of finely-pleated beige-tinted kasha, and her small feet and well-shaped legs were encased in high red Russia-leather boots.

Only the wearer's extraordinary slenderness made the fantastic costume look graceful, and even appropriate.

Cressida Daryl did not look cold or nipped by the wintry wind, as most women would have done, after the long open motor drive from London in December weather; for her head had been well wrapped up in a long soft grey veil, which she had unwound while the car raced up the drive.

The hall was brightly lit, and the newcomer stopped short when she saw the tall handsome young man standing by dumpy plain Lizzie Bowden.

"Hullo!" she exclaimed. "So this is the lucky man?"

She looked Larry Wortle up and down with a touch of insolent, as well as mirthful, interest. Then she added, after a moment's pause, "I congratulate you most heartily."

But this time it was not at the lucky man, it was at his bride-elect, that she smiled mischievously, as she uttered the ambiguous words.

Wortle began helping the lovely stranger to strip off her long fur coat, and as he did so he remained curiously silent. To use a colloquialism which was only then just coming into fashion, and which indeed Lizzie had never heard, he had fallen for Cressida at once.

Meeting the long ardent gaze of his compelling grey eyes, and noting the flush which had already mounted to his very handsome, if weak-chinned, face, the newcomer felt a thrill of gratified vanity.

Come, come! This was distinctly interesting.

Captain Wortle, stupid disagreeable little Lizzie Bowden's lover, promised sport – the only kind of sport in which Cressida Daryl took any real pleasure, and the only kind at which she was an expert. But then what an expert was she at what has been wittily called "the greatest of indoor games!"

As to any possible pain or distress which might result to Wortle's future wife, from the bit of sport she had just promised herself, Lady Bignor's enchanting young friend gave no thought at all. To beautiful, highly sophisticated Cressida Daryl, Lizzie Bowden was still only a tiresome overgrown child, unfairly dowered by fate with vast wealth which she had no notion how to use or enjoy.

While Alice Bignor's real niece had been at a fashionable girls' school, where poor Lizzie had learnt nothing of the only thing that really matters to a woman, the science of life, the adopted niece had spent many happy days in what she still called, to herself, dear Millhanger House.

Cressida Daryl's mother had died when she was three years old, and she had been brought up by a group of careless selfish relations, who had tossed her the one to the other as if she had been a pretty kitten. Then, before she was twenty, she had become involved, though only as a witness, in a notorious divorce case, and there had followed a bitter quarrel with her proud poor old-fashioned father.

Lady Bignor, kind, impulsive, and free to do what she liked, for Lizzie was safe at school, had taken the girl's part, as well as a warm liking for one who had then been so forlorn; and for some years Cressida had been encouraged to regard Millhanger House as her real home. But, as to that pleasant state of things, everything had altered after Lizzie Bowden had left school and come to live with her aunt.

The adopted niece had made the mistake of underestimating the real niece's very solid position in Lady Bignor's life, if not in her heart. And as Cressida Daryl, now fatherless as well as motherless, acquired more and more friends in the carefree hedonist world in which she delighted, and which so soon came to delight in her, she was less and less seen in the hospitable country house where she had once been a constant guest.

True, Cressida still called Lady Bignor "Aunt Alice," and confided to her such secrets concerning her life as could be told to her closest friend. And she still came to her, now and again, on a short visit. But, to use her own inward expression, life at Millhanger House, with Lizzie Bowden as sub-hostess, had become, at any rate to such a popular and fastidious person as herself, a crashing bore.

When she had first heard, a week ago, of Lizzie's engagement, she had thought of the girl's future husband with acrid contempt. What sort of a man could he be – this Larrymore Wortle – who was apparently eager to take on for life the utterly unattractive and pompous, as well as small-natured, Lizzie Bowden?

But now, in the fraction of a minute, Cressida Daryl's feeling for Larry Wortle changed from one of contempt to pity. Poor devil! Her first glance into his unusually good-looking, moody face, had told her that before he had sold himself into bondage – and such bondage – he must indeed have come to the end of his tether.

"A fellow feeling makes us wondrous kind;" though she had, up to now, kept the fact entirely to herself, Cressida was thinking very seriously, though with a most painful sensation of distaste and shrinking, of marrying a middle-aged man for whom she had not a vestige of real liking, still less of respect. But he was very very rich, and what he called his heart was her's. For a while at least, every whim would be indulged, every momentary longing, however fantastic, which possessed her, would be instantly gratified. His business interests compelled him to live four months of each year in Egypt, and Cressida, with many an inward shuddering feeling of revolt, had almost made up her mind to go out to Cairo this spring.

But nothing of what was in her mind showed in her lovely oval face and star-like eyes, as she stood in the hall of Millhanger House, smiling with a kind of queer sympathy and understanding at Larry Wortle, while her smart-looking luggage was being taken off the car.

The sudden appearance of the youth who had driven her down from town, and who was coming in to have tea before going off again, created a slight diversion.

He was an exceptionally ugly young man, his attitude towards Cressida one of humble adoration; and she did not even take the trouble to introduce him, while he shook hands with Lizzie Bowden.

Lizzie never allowed anyone to shirk even a trifling duty, if she could help it, and she had already assumed the part of joint-mistress of Millhanger House. So "Aunt Alice is not in yet; but tea will soon be coming to the drawing room. Will you please introduce your friend to me, Cressida?"

"I forgot you didn't know him, Lizzie! I thought everyone knew Piggy Burt? The vulgar would tell you that he's one of the best," and the speaker threw him a delightful smile.

Young Mr. Burt coloured with pleasure. In some ways his fleshy, pallid face might have reminded the unkind of a nice little pig. No doubt it was partly because he was so ugly that he adored Cressida Daryl. In her loveliness there was an ethereal quality that constantly attracted the grosser, more materialistic, elements about her.

When through the drawing room door Cressida made at once for the fire. Holding out her hands to the leaping flame, "How too divine!" she exclaimed.

While Lizzie was playing hostess to the young man whose nickname she now knew to be "Piggy," Larry Wortle swiftly, unobtrusively, followed the exquisite stranger across to the fireplace. And, as they stood there, side by side, for a few moments, neither uttered a word, though each was intensely conscious of the other's nearness.

At last, with a smile that was already full of intimate implications, Cressida Daryl, turning her head towards him, murmured, "Don't you find this house ideal for making love? Others found it so, when I used to be here so much with Alice Bignor, while Lizzie was still at school." Her voice sank still lower as she went on: "It was such a delicious, perfect place then! I suppose – I hope – it's like Heaven to you now?"

Wortle felt bewildered – bewildered and queerly moved. There had been something so mocking, even so malicious, in the way Miss Daryl had thrown her congratulations at him – or was it at Lizzie? – in the hall. But the words she had just whispered in that low, delicious voice, had sounded kind, gentle, sincere. Also there had been, in her lovely shadowed eyes, a glimmer of understanding and even, God help him, pity.

So it was that he made no answer to that half-question. Instead, hardly conscious that he was doing so, he drew yet nearer to the Undine-like stranger. It was as if he were being drawn towards Cressida Daryl by an invisible, but oh, how powerful and irresistible, a magic lure.

At last she moved a little back from the hot fire, and Wortle was now so close to her that – was it by design or chance? – he touched the fingers of the slender hand now hanging limply by her side.

But it was not by chance that his hand closed, with a strong caressing grip, over those delicate fingers.

An unkind critic, a man to whom she had certainly behaved very badly, for he had loved her devotedly, and for a short time she had allowed him to think that they would be married "some day," had once called Cressida a rogue elephant. But, when saying that, he had been blinded by pain and anger, for, apart from the rare perfection of her person, and the worldly-wise qualities which made her so agreeable a companion to such a woman as was Lady Bignor, she was a typical example of her age, and of the society of which she had become a cherished ornament.

Though far from physically strong, Cressida Daryl had deliberately cultivated in herself the precious twin gifts of good humour and high spirits. Also, with the possible exception of Lizzie Bowden, she had never made, even in extreme youth, the mistake of despising other women.

Cressida possessed many loyal friends of her own sex, especially among those young married women who were her contemporaries, or just a little older than herself. Most of them felt for her an indulgent fondness which made them forgive her only half-hidden selfishness, and her secret, fierce determination to secure the kind of refined luxury, and pleasant social surroundings, which alone made life tolerable to this little sister of the rich.

The discontented among her acquaintances envied her apparently luxurious, easy life, and it was true that her only serious troubles were connected with money. But in these days money, or rather the lack of money, can overshadow every other trouble. Cressida Daryl was always in debt, especially for clothes, and that though the leading dressmakers all liked her, and were well aware that, in exchange for an occasional frock, she brought them valuable custom.

But now, at long last, she was compelled to face the fact that it was becoming more and more difficult, nay impossible, for her to go on living the only life possible to one like herself, on the small income produced by the few thousand pounds which remained to her and which had been strictly tied up by her father. So strictly tied up that even her clever brain could devise no way by which they, too, could be squandered.

It was characteristic of Lizzie Bowden's habit of mind that it had not occurred to her to ask for tea to be brought in the moment the newcomers had arrived, tired and cold after their long drive. And, as the minutes slipped by, Cressida began to feel almost faint from fatigue. But at last the drawing room door opened; tea appeared; and the oddly-assorted party of four people gathered round the low tea table. Even so, the two strongly contrasted couples – Cressida Daryl and Larry Wortle, Lizzie Bowden and Piggy Burt – kept more or less together.

Young Burt got up at last, "I expect I ought to be going now," he said mournfully.

How he hated leaving this delightful house, where a jolly lot of people were apparently gathering together for Christmas, to say nothing of his own adored Cressida! She threw him a kindly glance. "My dear Piggy," she cried. "You can't go before you've seen Lady Bignor. I'm sure she'll want you to stay to dinner. At any rate, let's see if she does."

She stood up, and stretched her arms above her head. "Why shouldn't we put on the gramophone, and dance in the hall? That's what we did last year. D'you remember, Lizzie? It was quite good fun."

Yet, even as she uttered the words, she was remembering how exceedingly dull that little party, made up of the young folk belonging to the immediate neighbourhood, had seemed to her. But now that she was embarked on what she already knew was to be a secret exciting love adventure, she found herself looking forward to the next ten days, and no longer regretting the amusing house party with which she had expected to spend Christmas this year.

Cressida's quick, subtle mind had travelled a long, long way while she had waited, hungering, for her tea.

If she could make friends with attractive Captain Wortle, without making dull-witted Lizzie Bowden jealous – well, then, the young couple's future home, which she had already heard was to be in one of the hunting counties, might be a pleasant refuge for her now and again, that is, if she finally decided to give up all thought of marriage with the only man who just now was willing, nay eager, to marry her.

But could she so decide? Could she? *Could she?* She had never felt so anxious and uncertain about any question concerning the only thing that had ever really mattered to her – her own present and future existence.

She felt sure that Alice Bignor, one of the few people, indeed perhaps the only person in the world, who loved her unselfishly, would certainly advise her to try to stay the course.

But as to the goal?

Cressida Daryl was quite candid with herself. What she was always subconsciously seeking was a sufficiently well-born and agreeable, but above all, really rich man who would love her with an indulgent selfless fidelity, which he must be brought to understand could not be exacted from her.

Sometimes she wondered uneasily why this ideal mate seemed so hard to come by. Many of her contemporaries, with not a tithe of her beauty, her intelligence, and her charm, had succeeded in drawing from the strange lottery of life exactly such a husband. But life, to most human beings, is a balanced ration. Cressida Daryl had much – very much – that most women lack, and that many even fortunate women would give their souls to possess. With regard to her chances of making what in her world was called "a good marriage," Fate, so far, had not been kind.

3

AT HALF-PAST EIGHT THE next morning, Lizzie Bowden awoke to see her maid come noiselessly into the room, bringing her early cup of tea.

Smiling, the woman exclaimed, "Her ladyship thought you would like to see this paper, miss," and she laid a picture paper on the pink silk eiderdown.

Another kind of young lady, indeed almost any other young lady, would have said a word of thanks, or any rate "passed the time of day," as the maid, a few minutes later, resentfully observed in the servants' hall. But that was not this young lady's way.

Yet Lizzie felt happy, she even felt very happy, as she sipped her tea, and watched the curtains being drawn back on what had become, in the night, a world of snow.

"Aren't there any letters for me?" she asked, suddenly remembering that the news of her engagement had appeared in yesterday's morning papers.

"The letters won't be here before half-past nine, as it's so near to Christmas, miss."

Half-past nine? How dreadfully late! Aunt Alice ought to write and complain to the Postmaster-General. That was what she, Lizzie Bowden, would certainly do in her aunt's place. But Aunt Alice was always stupidly good-natured, and hated getting anyone into trouble, as she put it.

Then the girl told herself contentedly that, after all, it would be great fun opening her letters with Larry, after they had had their breakfast, and were settled down, alone together, for a blissful morning in the study.

Gazing through the window which was opposite to her bed, she noted with pleasure how heavy lay the snow on the branches of an evergreen oak.

Aunt Alice couldn't try to hunt her and Larry out of doors to take a tiresome walk this morning, especially as she, Lizzie, still had a cold.

How delicious to know her lover was here, under the same roof as herself!

They had been parted for nearly a week when he had arrived just before lunch yesterday. Though he had written to her every day, and such dear, loving, little letters, during those long cold days she had missed him horribly. Yes, that was the word – horribly.

All at once there came into her mind a sensation of annoyance at the thought that Cressida Daryl was also here, in Millhanger House, and going to stay such a long time, too, – till after the New Year.

Strangely enough – and it really was strange – Lizzie had never been jealous of Cressida. And yet perhaps it was not so very strange, after all – for why be jealous of a person for whom one feels a certain contempt, as well as a measure of strong disapproval?

Though she possessed quite a good working affection for her aunt, Lizzie had never been fond enough of Lady Bignor – the two were too utterly different the one from the other – for her to feel hurt at her aunt's affection for Cressida. She simply thought it foolish of Lady Bignor to be so attached to a selfish and affected girl, of whom all "nice people" expressed energetic disapproval.

By Lizzie Bowden, anything at all unusual, and especially anything exceptionally seductive, in a woman's manner, or even in her appearance, was always vaguely put down to affectation.

Still, she did tell herself this morning, and with a feeling of faint resentment, that her aunt needn't have allowed Cressida Daryl to come to Millhanger House just now.

Take last evening? If Cressida hadn't been here, she, Lizzie, would naturally have been the centre of interest, in view of her approaching marriage. As it was, Cressida, from the moment they had sat down to dinner, had done all the talking.

Chitter-chatter, chatter-chitter, telling so-called funny stories, some being quite horrid stories, about the queer people she knew. And Lady Bignor, even Colonel Slade, had evidently enjoyed hearing all the silly London gossip, and so, Lizzie suspected, had Larry.

There was something else which the girl also now remembered, with a feeling of growing exasperation.

After she had gone up to bed (Lizzie hated sitting up late) she had heard Larry and Cressida laughing and talking in the hall. And, quite an hour later, she had actually been wakened by the noise the two had made at the top of the staircase, at the end of the corridor, as they said goodnight.

Yes, it had been really very thoughtless of Aunt Alice to ask Cressida here just now. But Aunt Alice was "like that," impulsive and foolishly good-natured, and always allowing selfish people to make a convenience of her.

At last Lizzie opened languidly the picture paper lying on the eiderdown, and a slight smile lit up her face when she saw, on the inside sheet, a portrait of herself.

It was only a head cut out of a group which had been taken at Newmarket two years ago, when she was nineteen, and just beginning to go about by herself.

And then, all at once, came the unpleasant revelation that this stupid picture showed her at her worst, not best. Why hadn't the editor of the paper taken the trouble to procure a really nice photograph of her, instead of this horrid old thing?

Why, there was a picture of Cressida Daryl too – dressed more or less like a man, in a winter sports costume!

Now Cressida, as everyone who knew her was aware, had always been too delicate for any form of even the mildest outdoor game. So how extravagant of her to have bought these sports clothes, unless, as had once been said in Lizzie's presence, she got most of her clothes for nothing. This because Cressida was supposed to show them off, and because she recommended the dressmakers who had made her these valuable gifts to her unsuspecting friends – a vulgar, indeed scarcely an honest, thing to do.

Lizzie's pale lips curved in scorn as she looked more closely at the photograph of the elegant slender figure, silhouetted against a dead white background.

"It makes her look six feet high," she said to herself.

Then she glanced again at her own fat, blurred, pictured face. Surely she could never have looked like that?

There came over her a conscious hope that Larry would never see the hideous thing. All the more did she trust that he would never see it, as the words printed under the portrait both annoyed and offended her :-

"Miss Elizabeth Bowden, who, as will be noticed, still resists the shingling craze, is the only child of the late Major Burlington Bowden, of the Sixtieth. At his death, which occurred ten years ago, Major Bowden left his daughter three hundred and fifty-five thousand pounds. Miss Bowden has just become engaged to Captain Larrymore Wortle. Though not overmuch blessed with this world's goods, Captain Wortle is a keen sportsman, and one of the most popular young men in the smart set."

What an odd, disagreeable way of announcing her forthcoming marriage! Almost as if she, Lizzie, not being in the smart set, was about to buy a husband who was.

Cressida, undeniably, was in the smart set, and the fact that Larry had never met her till yesterday proved conclusively, at any rate to his future wife, that he was not.

That knowledge was at once mortifying and consoling.

Then she looked at what was written under the, in her eyes, almost indecent-looking picture of her aunt's pet: –

"An unconventional portrait of Miss Cressida Daryl, who has been described as the loveliest, the cleverest, and the best-dressed girl in "young" society. Miss Daryl is spending Christmas with the Duchess de Quérouailles, who has taken Altramont Castle for the hunting season."

Lizzie let the paper drop with a pettish gesture of disgust. Why, there wasn't one true word in the rot printed there!

To begin with, Cressida Daryl wasn't a girl any longer. She must be at least twenty-eight. As to her looks? Lizzie admitted reluctantly to herself that most people did think Cressida lovely. But they didn't realise how much of that spurious loveliness was due to clever "make-up," and the fact that Providence had endowed her with a short upper lip, tiny white teeth, and peculiar-looking, slanting green eyes.

If saying daring, sometimes quite improper, things, that make silly people laugh, is clever, then no doubt Cressida was clever in a way. But she, Lizzie Bowden, had often been shocked at Cressida's ignorance as to facts – about geography, to give only one example – that every well-educated person knows.

***

Breakfast at Millhanger House was served at what Lady Bignor called "an easy nine-thirty." But Lizzie, who had never given up her school habits of punctuality, came down just as the grandfather clock in the hall chimed out the half-hour.

She did not expect to see Larry yet awhile. Larry came down at all hours in the morning.

Before they had been actually engaged, Lizzie had been hurt by hearing a peppery old gentleman exclaim one day at breakfast in the country house where she and Larry were meeting for the second time, "Captain Wortle is the laziest young chap I ever struck!"

So there was no reason to hurry now.

This being so, while crossing the hall, the girl went over to the table where the letters were put out each morning.

For the first time in her life, Lizzie Bowden's pile of letters was far the largest. And there were also three registered parcels addressed to herself.

That must mean that certain folk, taking time by the fore-lock, had actually sent her their wedding presents yesterday, unless these were early Christmas gifts? In any case how awfully nice – and yes, how exciting.

She gathered up the envelopes, and counted them with child-ish glee. There were over twenty. But she wouldn't read even one of them yet. It would be far more fun to wait for Larry.

And then, as she opened the door of the dining room, Lizzie saw with astonishment that not only Larry, but Cressida, also, was already there – Cressida who always had her breakfast in bed.

The two who had come down so early had evidently already finished breakfast, for they were standing together, gazing out of one of the windows on to the snowy landscape.

Strangest of all, in a way, was the fact that Cressida was dressed for going out, and in the breeches and long sports coat in which she had been photographed. The breeches were dark brown, the coat was of yellow velveteen, bound with brown leather, and on their wearer's head was a yellow and brown peaked cap.

Lizzie's mind did not as a rule work very quickly, but it did, now, jump to the right conclusion; this was that Larry Wortle and Cressida Daryl must have arranged with one another, late last night, to go out together this morning. And, as she stood just inside the dining room door, before the two by the window had yet become aware of her presence, she made up her mind, quite definitely, that the plan made last night should miscarry.

With swelling anger she told herself that it was so like Cressida Daryl to try and grab the only young man in the party! But Lizzie, as the old saw says, knew a trick worth two of that.

The fire in the study had been lit at eight o'clock, so that she and Larry could spend a long happy morning there. It would take them quite all the morning, and perhaps part of the afternoon as well, to answer the thick bundle of letters she held clutched in her hand.

All at once Cressida turned round and saw her.

"Hullo, Lizzie! Up betimes as usual?"

There was a touch of mocking disdain in the soft clear voice.

How poor Lizzie longed to be able to say something smart and clever in reply! Something, for instance, implying how surprised *she* had been to find Cressida up betimes?

But Lizzie was not good at the uptake, so she remained silent, the while she went across to a side table, in order to choose herself something nice for breakfast.

As she came back, with a heaped-up plateful, Cressida Daryl observed, addressing no one in particular, "I telephoned Jack Danesborough before breakfast. He's just settled down at Birlings Place. He's asked me over to lunch, and I'm to bring anyone I like with me. He's got a splendid toboggan slide—"

She waited a moment; then, as Lizzie still said nothing, she added, "I hope you'll come too, if you're not afraid of making your cold worse?"

Then, at last, Lizzie spoke out. "Aunt Alice hasn't met Lord Danesborough yet. Neither have I. People say it bores him to know his neighbours. Besides, I don't think I could go and lunch in a man's house when I've never even seen him."

Cressida laughed, and it was not a pleasant laugh.

"Really, Lizzie, you're antediluvian! You ought to have been born eighty years ago, my dear. You belong to the wax-flower and glass-shade period."

Again poor Lizzie wished that she was as quick and sharp as Cressida always managed to be.

She longed – oh! how she longed – to put in witty language her view that whatever period she, Lizzie Bowden, belonged to, Cressida Daryl undoubtedly formed part of a horrid, vulgar set, who were always willing to eat dirt, if by so doing they could have a bit of what they called "fun."

However, she couldn't be really rude to one who was more or less her guest, as well as her aunt's. Also her mouth was rather full, so she simply shook her head, obstinately.

As for Larry, he had slipped, unobtrusively, from the room.

Cressida came close up to the dining table, and Lizzie noticed, with indignant interest, that she was made up more than usual – for the benefit of Larry, of course.

Fortunately Larry loathed all that sort of thing; he had spoken, only yesterday, and with cruel scorn, of a lady, designated by him as "an old trout," who made up a great deal.

But what was this Cressida was saying, while gazing down at her with those inscrutable pale green eyes which some foolish people thought her greatest claim to beauty?

"I like your young man, Eliza. I do hope you're kind to him?"

But before Lizzie could make up her mind how to answer that silly question, Lady Bignor came into the room.

"What's this I hear?" – she was looking at both girls— "that Larry has hired a two-seater in the village? He needn't have done that! There's the old motor standing idle in the garage to which he would be welcome—"

Lizzie stared at her aunt. Larry couldn't have hired a two-seater from the village without telling her, his fiancée. Besides, why should he have thought of doing such a thing? Someone must have made a stupid mistake.

And then Cressida intervened, and made what was for her quite a long speech.

"We've all been asked to go over to Birlings Place, Aunt Alice," she said coolly. "Jack Danesborough has made a splendid toboggan slide – and he's longing for some of us to go over and try it. That's why Captain Wortle thought it would be a good plan to make an arrangement with the local garage, so that he can have a two-seater whenever he feels like it."

Then Cressida was at the bottom of this? Lizzie looked at her with indignant surprise.

"If the snow lies," went on Cressida, "two of us, at any rate, might go over every day. Jack Danesborough has got a most amusing Christmas party, and tobogganing is such fun! He telephoned me this morning, and said I was to bring as many as I liked to lunch. So I hope you'll come, and Colonel Slade, too, of course."

"I don't want to speak ill of your friend, my dear, but Lord Danesborough has let it be known that he doesn't want to know his neighbours – a most impertinent thing for a young man to give out!"

Lady Bignor spoke with far more heat than usual. "I know that George Slade hasn't even met him yet, and I don't think either George or I would care to go to a man's house before we've seen him."

"Just what I said," observed Lizzie eagerly.

It was pleasant to find Aunt Alice on her side, for once.

"Jack's still only camping at Birlings Place," said Cressida defensively. "I hope you won't mind our going over there this morning – I mean Captain Wortle and I?"

Lady Bignor looked at her uncertainly. "You mean for lunch?"

"Yes, for lunch."

Then Lizzie's aunt caught a glimpse of Lizzie's lowering face.

"Oh, but I forgot! Captain Wortle can't go any distance this morning," she said decidedly.

"He himself arranged that our lawyer should telephone him between twelve and one – about something important to do with Lizzie's marriage settlement."

"Then will you be so kind as to send me over to Birlings Place alone, Aunt Alice?"

Cressida spoke with her usual easy-going nonchalance.

"It isn't easy for me to do that this morning, I've promised to take Mrs. Lancaster in to Guildford."

There was a moment's pause. Then Cressida went over to the curtained door, and so into the hall.

"Captain Wortle!"

Lizzie and Lady Bignor heard, from the dining room, the eager answer. "Yes, Miss Daryl?"

"Could you run me over to Birlings Place? Aunt Alice says you've got to be here for a telephone call about twelve. But there'll be plenty of time for you to take me there, and get back, before then."

Lady Bignor hurried off into the hall, and Lizzie, who by now was standing up in her place at the breakfast table, heard her aunt exclaim,"No, no, that won't do! Mr. Coxe may telephone any time after ten o'clock."

Lizzie left her breakfast, and followed her aunt into the hall.

For the first time in her life she threw Lady Bignor a look of real affection and gratitude.

"I've a tremendous lot of letters to show you, Larry," she began eagerly, "and some of them must be answered before the twelve o'clock post."

The young man was standing by the front door, and outside it, in the snow, there already stood the shabby little two-seater. He had evidently gone and brought it round from the garage, on leaving the dining room.

Even Lizzie could see how angry and how disappointed he looked. But that only made her the more determined to have her own way.

As for Lady Bignor, she was one of those sensible women who are never ashamed of changing their minds or their plans at a moment's notice.

"I'll take Mrs. Lancaster out this afternoon, and the motor can take you to Birlings at once, Cressida. It's too cold for an open motor," she exclaimed.

Cressida smiled affectionately at her hostess. She felt faintly amused. Perhaps, after all, it would be better fun to arrive alone, this first time, at Birlings Place?

"Thanks so much, Aunt Alice. I'm quite ready to start now. I simply adore tobogganing. It's so exciting."

She lifted her beautiful fur coat off the oak chest on which it was lying.

"I'll walk round to the garage, now, and tell Stevens you say he may drive me over. It's only a very few miles, isn't it? He could be back in time to take you to Guildford – at least I think so. I'm sure Jack Danesborough can send me back."

Larry Wortle was now standing facing the three ladies, his face, as Lady Bignor told herself, like a thunder cloud. He sprang forward, brushing past Lizzie almost rudely; then he helped Cressida on with her coat and, opening the front door, shut it quickly behind the two of them.

"I had no idea Cressida knew Lord Danesborough so well; I wonder if he likes her?" observed Lady Bignor musingly. "She's evidently mad keen to go over to Birlings Place as often as possible. That's why she's made Larry hire that absurd two-seater."

"I've always heard her say she hated open motors. But I expect she finds us a very dull party," said Lizzie sorely.

Lady Bignor gave a quick glance at her niece. She was already uncomfortably aware that Cressida Daryl did not find Larry Wortle dull; but the longer Lizzie remained ignorant of that fact, the better.

"If I'd known she was coming for Christmas, I'd have got an extra man!" she exclaimed. "But I didn't know, and it's too late now. We shall have to try and get Lord Danesborough over, as Cressida seems to like him so much."

The girl walked across the hall to the big window, and, looking out, she shivered a little.

"I'm sure that Larry will be much more comfortable lunching here, with us and Uncle George, than going over to Birlings Place, Aunt Alice."

Again, Lady Bignor threw a quick look at her niece. Was it possible that Lizzie really thought that such a man as Larry Wortle would prefer a quiet luncheon with his fiancée, her aunt, and a middle-aged man, to an amusing luncheon with Lord Danesborough and his lively young house party?

There came over the older woman an unwonted feeling of tenderness for the bride-to-be. Poor foolish child! How little she knew of life, and how very, very little she knew of men. She remembered how happy, how contented, Lizzie had looked yesterday. But Lizzie did not look happy or contented now. There was a puzzled, sullen, discontented, look on her face. And oh, dear! What an ugly frock she had on.

The frock was green, with dark red diagonal stripes across the jumper. A model sports garment which had been a marvellous bargain. Lizzie's aunt told herself that it would have been dear at any price, and would have made Venus herself look thick and plain.

And then, all at once, there came over Lady Bignor a feeling of misgiving with regard to Cressida Daryl.

Had she done a foolish thing in consenting to have so attractive a creature here just now? Then, with a sensation of relief, she reminded herself that Cressida Daryl was no fool. Cressida must be very well aware that, with regard to Larry Wortle, she must, as a matter of course, keep off the grass. All the same, she did not feel quite happy. Why didn't that foolish young man come indoors again? It was not his business to play host to Cressida.

She put her hand, with a kindly gesture, on her niece's shoulder.

"Why, you haven't yet opened even one of your letters, child!"

"I want to open them with Larry," answered Lizzie in a low voice. "He said yesterday he'd love to see them all; and he showed me two or three that he'd had from people who already knew about our engagement. They were awfully nice letters, Aunt Alice; they all said what a very lucky man he was."

"So he is," said Lady Bignor briskly. "A very lucky man indeed. In the old days, before you were engaged, I often told George Slade that you'd make a splendid little wife some day to a lucky man! You've some fine qualities, my dear. For one thing, you're so loyal—"

"Am I?" said the girl wistfully, "I hope I am."

"I looked into the study on my way down," went on Lady Bignor. (What could that young fool be doing outside, and without a coat on, too?) "There's a splendid fire, and you two will be as warm as toast in there, and as happy, I hope, as two love-birds."

Lizzie blushed, a deep, unbecoming blush; and Lizzie's aunt reminded herself a little ruefully that there had always been something queerly reserved and secretive about her niece – a secretiveness of nature which had come to her from a shy, nervous mother who, like Lizzie herself, had been an heiress. Lizzie's father had been a very normal type of his class and upbringing – good-humoured, easy-going, and frank.

Slowly the girl, her unopened letters in her hand, made a move towards the dining room door. And then she stood still, as if she didn't quite know what to do next.

"You'd better go into the drawing room, or, better still, into the study," said Lady Bignor a little impatiently. None of these three selfish self-absorbed young people had given a thought to the fact that she had not yet had her breakfast.

"Larry won't be long now," she resumed. "I suppose he's gone round to put that horrid little hireling back into our garage."

"I suppose he has," said Lizzie, in a low voice and on the edge of tears.

She was so afraid that, after all, Cressida Daryl would force Larry to go with her to Birlings Place! Once there he would certainly be made to stay on to lunch, and her whole day would be spoilt.

It was with deep relief that both aunt and niece saw the front door slowly opening, while their own motor flashed past the house.

As Larry Wortle came into the hall, there was a peculiar expression on his good-looking face, and for a moment his hostess, who had caught that look, felt that she hated him.

"Well?" he said flippantly, "here I am! Duty calls, and I obey—"

"By no means," said Lady Bignor sharply. "It was by your wish, and your wish alone, Larry, that Mr. Coxe arranged to call you up this morning. It is also owing to you that all the arrangements with regard to Lizzie's marriage settlement are going through as quickly as possible."

She waited a moment, then added more lightly, "I've never believed in the present mania for short engagements."

The young man made no answer to that observation, and she went on, this time speaking in a cold decided tone.

"Would you like me to put a call through to Mr. Coxe to say that there's no hurry, after all, about the marriage settlement, and that we'll wait to discuss certain points till after the New Year? After all, you and Lizzie only became officially engaged yesterday. In some ways it might be better to fix the wedding day in March, rather than in February."

Larry Wortle gave a sideways glance at Lizzie Bowden's aunt; and perhaps there was that in her shrewd, good-looking face which frightened him, and brought him back, sharply, to his bearings.

Flinging back his head, "You quite misunderstood me, Lady Bignor!" he exclaimed. "Of course I want everything to be hurried up. As far as I'm concerned I'd like to be married tomorrow—"

He took Lizzie's hand in his with a furtive movement, and Lizzie gave those strong fingers a grateful squeeze. She couldn't think why Aunt Alice had just spoken in such a very disagreeable way – and as if it really didn't matter at all when they were married! She, too, though it wouldn't be maidenly to say so, would be more than pleased to be married tomorrow. . .

Lizzie's resentment against Lady Bignor endured throughout the whole morning, for her lover had evidently been greatly hurt and offended.

When the two were settled down, alone at last, in the warm, comfortable study, Larry's irritation continued for a long time; and, after she had, as she put it to herself, soothed him down, he was quite unlike his usual attentive, agreeable self. He even yawned once or twice, when reading certain gushing letters from his future wife's old schoolfellows, some of whom she had entirely lost sight of, but who apparently had not forgotten her, and who now showed great interest in her forthcoming marriage.

A little after midday came the London telephone call.

Larry was away a long time answering it; and when he came back into the study, Lizzie could see that the conversation with her lawyer had ruffled him.

"Do tell me what Mr. Coxe said?" she asked eagerly.

Everything to do with money, and the disposal of money, held a real interest for Lizzie Bowden. Her maternal grandfather had been a great Victorian contractor, a man who, starting from nothing, had left each of his seven children over a quarter of a million pounds. Two of these children, maiden ladies both, were still alive, but a day would come when this granddaughter of his would be quite twice as rich as she was now.

"Your Mr. Coxe is a damned suspicious chap," said Larry Wortle shortly.

"Suspicious?" Lizzie felt puzzled. "How do you mean, darling?"

"He is determined to tie up your capital even more tightly than it was tied up when you were a child," said the young man sharply. "But as I'm a pauper – worse luck! – I had to keep my thoughts as to the damned impertinent way he spoke to me, to myself."

Lizzie was a good deal concerned. She had never heard her lover speak in that rough, savage, tone of voice, before.

"Of course you can say anything in the world you like to me," she exclaimed, and there was a pathetic, yearning tone in her young voice.

"That wouldn't cut much ice," he said rudely. "From what I can make out you're completely in the hands of your lawyers."

"Indeed I'm not!" And she felt really nettled. "If you want to know the truth—"

She waited a moment, then she went on, speaking quickly, defensively, " – Mr. Coxe was determined that I shouldn't settle that thousand a year on you. He said there was no necessity for it, as I could make you an allowance. But I said, 'No, you were to have it!' And in my will, the will that I'm to sign on our wedding day—" She stopped; there had come a hard, painful lump in her throat, " – I've left you, I've left you – everything I've got."

"You're a brick, and I'm a brute," he said in a moved tone. And, at that moment, Larry Wortle meant what he said.

He got up; and she got up too, while slow, reluctant tears were rolling down her cheeks.

He put his arm round her. "Don't let's talk any more about money! I was a beast to speak to you as I did just now. I ought to have kept the insulting things that caddish attorney said to me, to myself. But to tell you the truth, darling, your aunt irritated me this morning. I can see she thinks I'm nothing but a fortune-hunter. And it's damnably unfair—"

He was kissing her now, for the first time that morning.

And, as she sat on his knee, silent as was her way when deeply moved, Lizzie's mind went back to the wonderful day when they had first met in a country house where she scarcely knew the hostess, a lady called Mrs. Berwick Jones.

How happy she had been, during those few days when no one, not even Aunt Alice and kindly George Slade, knew of the marvellous thing which was coming into her life! Larry's love had filled her heart, under that alien roof, not only with a kind of fairyland radiance, but with what she had never till then experienced in her, if opulent, still work-a-day, world, – real happiness.

Lizzie shuddered inwardly, sometimes, when she remembered how very nearly she had refused Mrs. Berwick Jones's invitation. It was her aunt who had forced her to accept it, and she had unwillingly consented to go, not agreeing at all with the remark, "After all, child, you must see new people sometimes?"

At once, so Larry had assured her again and again, when she had come down just before dinner the first evening, feeling ever so nervous and shy, he had felt drawn to her. Tremendously so in fact!

How strange to recall that at the time of that first meeting she had hardly noticed him at all. Lizzie had been by way, just then, of not liking men, and of being quite "off" marriage.

One middle-aged man, who had proposed to her this last summer, had said she should be his dear little pal. Pal!

Even since then, another, younger, man, had begged her earnestly to marry him, while actually admitting that he didn't love her. He had, however, promised to give her a good time; and she had answered, quick for once, "With my money, I suppose?"

But Larry had fallen in love with her in the good old way. No wonder that she found her Heaven in his arms.

All at once the young man looked at his watch, "It's time we started, isn't it – even if they do lunch at a quarter to two?"

She slipped off his knee, and standing up, gazed at him with surprise.

"Oh, but we're not going to Birlings Place. I thought it would be so nice, having lunch here quietly with Aunt Alice and Uncle George?"

She saw his face cloud over, and there rose from her heart a generous impulse – the impulse of the woman who loves – to make the loved one happy in his own way.

"You go over to Birlings Place by yourself, darling. I really don't feel up to it. My cold is getting worse every minute."

Come? This was distinctly sporting of her.

"I expect you're wise not to go out; it looks as if it's going to snow again. But I'm awfully sorry, sweetheart."

He tried to look really sorry, and he flattered himself, rightly, that he succeeded.

"But don't be too late back!" she urged. "I'm sure to have a lot more letters by the half-past one post; and I do so enjoy answering them with your help. You're so much cleverer than I am at all that sort of thing—"

A few minutes later Larry was off, comfortably ensconced in the shabby hireling, for Birlings Place, while his fiancée waved her hand to him through the great window in the hall.

What would Lizzie Bowden have felt could she have heard the words her lover actually uttered aloud, as he spun down the steep, snow-covered drive?

"How glorious, glorious, glorious to be out of that stuffy study – and away from that poor little girl!"

The old two-seater had never had more taken out of her. Already Larry Wortle longed, with a terrible longing, for Cressida Daryl.

For just her presence in a room; for her delicate, alluring nearness; for the sound of her curiously individual, seductive voice; most of all perhaps for a repetition of the long, measuring, mysterious, look she had cast on him this morning, when no others had been by. It was a look that seemed to say, in the wordless language of passion, that already there was an invisible, secret, link between them.

As the light little car slithered over the snowy ice-bound Surrey roads Larry Wortle lived over and over again what had happened last evening.

Lady Bignor and Colonel Slade had slipped away, after Lizzie had gone to bed with her cold, to play a game of billiards; and he and Cressida stayed on in the drawing room alone, talking together, at first about nothing in particular, then more intimately.

Soon he had found himself telling her all sorts of things about his past life, things which he had never felt inclined to tell anybody before. And Cressida, angel that she was, had allowed him to hold her hand, nay, her two hands, while he made his confession.

Their "friendship" had made giant strides in that wonderful hour.

At last she had gone over to one of the windows, and opened the curtains.

"It's snowing heavily, now. I hoped it would. I love a snowy Christmas!"

And then she had come back to where he was now standing, too moved, too much under the spell of her enchantment, to speak.

Then she had asked him suddenly, "Do you know Lord Danesborough?" And, as if waking from a dream, he had answered hesitatingly, as was his wont when asked that sort of question.

"I think I've met him once or twice – but I'm not sure."

"He's come into a very nice property, not far from here, called Birlings Place, and last time I saw him he told me there was a bit of ground in his park which would make a perfect toboggan slide. I mean to telephone tomorrow morning to know if we can go over and try it."

Hardly knowing what he was saying, he had exclaimed. "How splendid!"

Lord Danesborough was one of the leaders of the set to which he had always longed to belong – the set to which Cressida did belong.

His new friend had then asked him another question: "Can you drive a motor?"

Eagerly he had answered, "At one time I had the jolliest little two-seater in the world! But I had to sell her, worse luck, about four months ago, when I was desperately hard up."

"I suppose that was before you met Lizzie?" There had come a mocking cruel inflection into the gentle voice, and that had brought him to earth with a thud. By gad it had!

But soon he had been up in the clouds again, for, "Why don't you hire a two-seater while you're here; I know there's a garage in the village?" And he had seen in her eyes the unspoken words, the promise, "If you do that, we two shall be independent, both of managing Lady Bignor and of tiresome little Lizzie!"

No wonder that he had answered eagerly, "I'll get up early, and get through to the garage at once."

"If it's left off snowing in the morning, and we go over to Birlings Place, of course we'll stay to lunch."

She had added, a little awkwardly, "I don't think Lizzie will be up to such an expedition. She hates going out when she's got a cold."

As he said nothing to that, and only looked at her, his eyes aflame: "Well, time for bed, I suppose? We needn't go into the billiard room. They won't want to be disturbed," and she had smiled a mischievous little smile.

Together, and now talking eagerly, they had gone up the staircase leading from the hall to the one other storey of Millhanger House.

Then, remembering, she had put her finger to her lips. "Hush! I don't want Lizzie to hear us. This is the corridor we used to call 'The Maiden's Prayer,' in the old days." Dropping her voice still more, she had added, "If it's fine, can you be down to breakfast by nine?"

"At six if you like! How I wish we could stay up all night—"

For an hour or more, after leaving her, he had tortured himself with the thought that perhaps a little more courage on his part might have won him the kiss for which he had longed as the wanderer in the desert longs for the sound of running water.

4

"It's awfully pretty, Lucy! I do think it's kind of you and Major Mandeville to have given it to me, especially as it belonged to your mother."

Lizzie Bowden spoke with far more warmth of manner than was usual with her. In her hand she held, open, a shabby little jewel case containing a fine old-fashioned sapphire-and-pearl pendant.

She and Lucy Mandeville, the girl who was to be her one bridesmaid, were standing together in her bedroom.

Major Mandeville was a poor man, or at any rate he thought himself so. He and his daughter spent their lives trekking as he called it, from one golf hotel to another – not a pleasant or lively life for Lucy, but that thought never occurred to Lucy's father.

He, Colonel Slade, and Major Bowden had been subalterns together, so the friendship of the two girls was an hereditary friendship, and Lizzie liked small, fair-haired, pink-and-white Lucy better than she liked anyone else of her own age. It was she, who so seldom did anything on impulse, who had asked her aunt yesterday to send a telephone message asking the father and daughter to come over from the hotel where they were staying, some ten miles away, to spend a night at Millhanger House.

Major Mandeville, true to form, had managed to get in a round of golf this afternoon, in spite of the melting snow. So Lady Bignor had sent her motor for them after tea, and Lucy had come straight to Lizzie's bedroom to deliver her wedding gift.

And very graciously had Lizzie received the gift. Indeed, just a little to her own surprise, she felt something akin to real affection for Lucy today.

She was vexed with herself, now, remembering that Aunt Alice had thought of asking the Mandevilles to spend Christmas with them, as Christmas in an hotel must be so horrid.

But at the time she, Lizzie, had thrown cold water on the kindly suggestion. She had supposed there would be at Millhanger House what a French governess she had once had described as a *partie carrée*; that is, just Aunt Alice, George Slade, Larry Wortle, and herself.

But fate had ordained otherwise, and it would have been so much pleasanter to be a party of seven, than just to have two visitors – Cressida, to whom Larry had to be nice, and George Slade, to whom Aunt Alice liked to be nice. It made Lizzie sometimes feel, what she had never felt before when at home, "the odd man out," though really it was Cressida who was in that uncomfortable position.

It was unlucky, too, that Major Mandeville had an old friend joining him and Lucy tomorrow, so they could not remain on, as they had just been asked to do, for two more nights.

"I wish you could have stayed till Christmas Eve, Lucy; I do want you to make friends with Larry!" she exclaimed.

"I'm longing to see Captain Wortle. It must be great fun – being engaged?"

There was a wistful tone in the other girl's voice, but Lizzie took no note of that.

"It is rather fun," and there swept up into her face a hot, almost purple flush.

"I suppose you haven't begun to think about your trousseau, yet?"

"Indeed I have! I bought a lot of lovely things at the sales last week – I mean at the good sales of course. I don't see why one should throw money away, just because one's got some, do you, Lucy?"

As Lucy made no answer to that remark, for she could not imagine herself in a position to throw money away, Lizzie went on: "Aunt Alice wanted me to have coloured underthings – but I like pure white, don't you?"

She waited a moment, then added, "They're just behind you, in that cupboard. You can look at them if you like."

Lucy Mandeville turned round and eagerly opened the wide doors of a Sheraton gentleman's wardrobe which had belonged to Lizzie's father.

Lucy was a very old-fashioned girl, so "How lovely!" she cried sincerely. Then, "I suppose Captain Wortle is interested in every little thing about you?"

Lizzie did not answer the half-question. Instead, she moved over to the other side of the room and stood, as she sometimes did stand, doing nothing – unless thinking is doing something. Her mind had gone back, with justified resentment, to what had happened yesterday.

About four o'clock, when Larry and Cressida should have been coming back from Birlings Place, the chauffeur of an empty car had brought a note, addressed to Lady Bignor, explaining that Lord Danesborough had asked her two guests to stay on to dinner. So might Cressida's evening things, and those of Captain Wortle, be sent over?

And that wasn't all! The two had come back – well, you could only call it in the early hours of the morning, long after one o'clock.

Colonel Slade had let them in, for of course neither of them had a latchkey, and Aunt Alice hadn't liked the parlourmaid to sit up. She, Lizzie, had also stayed awake, feeling she couldn't really settle down till they were home again. No wonder poor Larry had been tired and cross all today.

Not that Lizzie had seen very much of her lover, for when she, herself tired and cross, had come down after having had her breakfast in bed, she had learnt from the parlourmaid that Captain Wortle was motoring Miss Daryl to a house some miles away. Some friends of Miss Daryl's were now living there – stupid people, who hadn't a telephone.

Cressida had stayed with her friends to lunch, but Larry had returned, though if it hadn't been that Aunt Alice insisted on sending the car, he would have gone back for Cressida in his horrid two-seater. Cressida Daryl – it was an outrage – was simply using Larry Wortle as her chauffeur!

With a smouldering feeling of anger, Lizzie told herself that this was why he and she had only had one hour together today – an hour spent, too, in such a horrid way, tramping along the high road at the bottom of the hill.

Aunt Alice had forced them to go out of doors, though Larry, like Lizzie herself, hated taking a constitutional.

They hadn't had much to say to one another during that stupid walk, though Larry had brightened up when he fell to talking about Birlings Place. He had explained what an amusing house it was, and what a jolly time he and all Lord Danesborough's other visitors had had the evening before – playing one of those gambling games at which, so Lizzie unfortunately remembered, Lady Bignor had once said one could lose quite a lot of money.

Foolishly she had asked Larry if they had played for money, and he had answered sharply, "Of course we did!"

And then she had asked a further unwise question—"Did you lose or win, darling?" And he had turned on her, "Come, Lizzie? As I'm so lucky in love, you know I must be unlucky at play."

More than that he had refused to say, but it had made her feel unhappy, suspicious, uncomfortable. Full of a nervous fear, too, that she might be going to marry a gambler. She had had, however, the sense to keep that fear to herself.

At last they had met the car coming back, and Cressida had given them a welcome lift home.

The rest of the afternoon had been spent by Larry in writing letters in his bedroom. Lizzie had tried to make him come into the study and answer them there, but he had refused, almost rudely, saying that he would be more comfortable by himself. He had added that he hated writing letters, especially answers to letters of congratulation; it was so difficult to know what to say without making a damn fool of oneself.

How she longed, how she ached, for Larry now! Surely he must be longing, aching, for her too?

There came back to the girl the memory of a blissful evening some time back, before their then half-understanding had been revealed even to Lady Bignor.

He, still Captain Wortle to them all, had been staying here, one of a small house party, and about half-past six, he had whispered to her, "Do dress quickly and come down early, little pet! Then we'll be able to have a jolly time alone together in the drawing room, before the others come down."

Tremulous with excitement, and feeling almost wicked, she had obeyed him, slipping down to the drawing room about half-past seven. There, by the fire, she had waited, her heart pounding in her bosom, for what had seemed a long time. But only two or three minutes had gone by before the door opened. Boldly her lover, still then her secret lover, had turned out the lights, and rushing across the room had taken her in his arms...

Why shouldn't she send Larry a little note to his room now, suggesting that they should do the same thing this evening? She had an excuse – a telegram containing congratulations on her marriage, coupled with an invitation to them both, from a great aunt on her mother's side of her family.

Answering her own question as she wished it answered, she turned to her friend and said quickly, "I'm afraid I must shoo you away now, Lucy. I've got such an awful lot of letters to write."

"You must have, dear; I'll go and unpack—"

But though she shut the wardrobe, and took a step towards the door, Lucy Mandeville lingered.

"I'm so excited at the thought of seeing Cressida Daryl!" she exclaimed.

"I don't see why you should be?"

"It's all very well for you to say that, Lizzie, as you've always known her. But she's quite a celebrated character. I saw in some paper last week that she'd had a wonderful offer to go on the films."

"I don't believe it," said Lizzie sharply. "If that was true I'm sure she'd have taken it, for she's fearfully fond of money."

"Perhaps she hasn't got a film face," said Lucy. She added, half to herself, "If I thought I had a film face I'd run away and go in for it."

"Lucy!" Lizzie Bowden looked, and felt, extremely shocked.

"Father's so old-fashioned he wouldn't dream of my doing such a thing. In fact he thinks it's almost indelicate of any lady to try and earn her own living; yet I often wish we were even poorer than we are, Lizzie—"

And, after that unwonted outburst, Lucy quickly left the room.

Lizzie hurried to her writing table. Without sitting down she bent over and scrawled across a piece of paper, "Do come down early, darling. I'll be in the drawing room by half-past seven. I've something to tell you."

Putting her note into an envelope, she rang the bell for her maid. "This is for Captain Wortle. Will you see that he gets it at once? It's very important. And you needn't come back, Gledding. I can manage quite well tonight."

"I'll just put out your things, miss."

"No, you needn't do that. I'll see to everything myself."

As the maid left the room, the clock in the hall struck seven.

Larry was leisurely in his ways, but even he could surely be ready by the time the dressing bell rang? That would give them a precious half hour, alone together downstairs.

Lizzie dressed far more quickly than usual, putting on the frock she had worn on the evening she remembered so well. It was a striking, dead-white frock, but, oddly enough, her aunt didn't like to see her in it. However, she liked it herself, and, what was far more important, Larry had said he thought it lovely.

She waited – just like that other time – till after the dressing bell had rung, and everyone had had time to disappear into their several bedrooms. Then she walked on tip-toe down the corridor, past the room where Cressida Daryl had been resting ever since she came in, and where she was now, no doubt, languidly beginning to dress for dinner.

Lizzie frowned as she passed that door, remembering the silly way sensible Lucy Mandeville had spoken of Cressida.

Running downstairs, she opened the drawing room door...

There all was still in darkness, save for the fitful shooting flames of the fire. Deliberately, she omitted to turn on the lights.

Suddenly, as she advanced into the dark room, she gave a stifled cry of surprise, for someone was lying back in a deep chair drawn up close to the fender.

Walking quickly back to the door, she turned on two of the electric lamps which stood on a table near the curtained windows.

And then? And then a sensation of genuine disgust, as well as of amazement, filled her mind. For a moment she felt, in very truth, as if she couldn't believe her eyes. But some obscure instinct impelled her to remain quite quiet and calm, and "You did startle me, Cressida," she observed.

"You're down very early, Lizzie?"

There was a slight edge of anxiety in Cressida's soft voice. But Lizzie was far too surprised, as well as too shocked, to notice that, for once, Cressida spoke to her simply, pleasantly.

She answered a little breathlessly, "I thought I'd come down early, as Lucy Mandeville is here; but I've forgotten my handkerchief."

Turning, she walked towards the door, and Cressida, still calling a truce, said plaintively, "You might put out the lights, if you don't mind, darling? My eyes ache so..."

In a whirl of inward indignation, and protest, Lizzie rushed upstairs. But when on the balcony overlooking the hall which ran round the upper storey of Millhanger House, she waited in some uncertainty.

What if Larry, in obedience to her behest, now appeared on his way to the drawing room? If he did that, she must think of some good excuse to send him back to his own room.

But Larry did not emerge from the further wing of the house where his bedroom was situated, and Lizzie at last began walking round the balcony leading to Lady Bignor's room.

Knocking on the door with impatient knuckles, she opened it and called out, "May I come in, Aunt Alice?"

"Of course, my dear! What's the matter?"

There was a tone of surprise in Lady Bignor's voice, for Lizzie very seldom came to her aunt's bedroom. It wasn't her way.

The girl pushed open the door, then she shut it carefully behind her, and waited a moment, nervously clasping and unclasping her hands.

Lady Bignor was standing before her very charming dressing table; she had on a becoming rose-red muslin dressing jacket, and she was brushing out her long, still abundant, hair.

"Aunt Alice—"

"Yes?" The other turned round. "My dear child, whatever is the matter? You look as white as a sheet!"

"Something's happened that I think will shock Major Mandeville, to say nothing of Uncle George, very, very much," said Lizzie in a stifled voice.

Lady Bignor felt disturbed; she put the brush that she was holding down on the dressing table. "Well?" she said rather impatiently, "well? What is it? Don't frighten me—"

"It's Cressida," gasped out Lizzie. "I can't tell you how horrid she looks. She's dressed just like a man!"

"Like a man, Lizzie? What do you mean?"

"I suppose she'd call it a pyjama suit, and, and – all I can say is that it's horribly indecent!"

And then, as she saw a slight smile coming over her aunt's face, she said sullenly, "However, perhaps you won't mind."

"Of course I shall mind very much if Cressida is wearing anything that really looks – well, horrid."

She glanced at her wristwatch, and saw that it was twenty minutes to eight.

"I don't suppose there's anyone about," she said reflectively. "And if there is, it won't hurt them to see me in my dressing gown for once," and she flung a wrap round her.

They both went out of the room, and round the open balcony, till they came to the corridor which, according to Cressida Daryl, had once been called 'The Maiden's Prayer.' And then Lizzie suddenly put her hand, with a hard grip, on her aunt's soft arm. "Not there," she whispered quickly. "Cressida is downstairs, in the drawing room."

"Downstairs? In the drawing room already?"

Lady Bignor felt a little bewildered, a little suspicious – she hardly knew of what. For the first time she asked herself why her niece, also, had dressed so early this evening.

When they were both in the hall, and just outside the drawing room door, she said quickly, "If you don't mind, Lizzie, I'd rather you went back to your own room till the dinner bell rings. I'd rather not scold Cressida in front of you – whatever it is she has done, or not done."

Lizzie made no spoken objection to that. Indeed, how could she? But she went up the stairs slowly, and a thought rebelliously.

Lady Bignor opened the drawing room door and turned up the light.

"My dear Alice, —" Cressida often dropped the "aunt" when the two were alone together. "What *is* the matter?"

The speaker rose, as she spoke, from the deep chair in which she had been lying back.

If a startling, she looked a very lovely, sight, in her Venetian-red peg-top trousers, her long Regency coat of the same material bound with dull gold braid, and her silvered gold waistcoat.

Lady Bignor ran forward and put her arm round her young friend's slender shoulders.

"My dear," she exclaimed, "you look – well, wonderful! But I'm afraid I must ask you to go upstairs and dress all over again. Jack Mandeville would have ten fits if he saw you; and as for George—?"

"What a pair of old fogies they must be." But she spoke quite good-humouredly. "Jack Mandeville, as you call him, has always been a narrow-minded, selfish old brute; and as for George Slade? – I thought he was like the old lady's pug who never had a naughty thought!"

"Did you indeed?" said her friend drily.

Cressida spun round and lightly kissed Lady Bignor on the cheek.

"Come, come, Alice! You know as well as I do that though faithful George might be shocked to see me dressed like this, he'd love to see you in the very spit of it – as my old nanny used to say."

As Lady Bignor grew a little pink, Cressida went on, eagerly, for her,

"It's La Boule's newest model – and you can have it to copy for your honeymoon. For of course you're going to have a honeymoon – worse luck for me! If you'll have it carried out in citron yellow and dull silver, darling, you'll look – well, quite divine."

"What d'you take me for? A vain old goose? Only your figure can carry off such a – I really don't know what to call it!"

"Its French name is 'L'Hermaphrodite,'" said Cressida demurely.

"And its English name?"

"'Little Lord Fauntleroy,' I should think."

Lady Bignor laughed – then, "Quick!" she cried, "You haven't very long – a bare quarter of an hour," but her tone was kindly and indulgent.

"I suppose that little cat Lizzie gave me away?" said Cressida.

They were walking together towards the door; and then, suddenly, Lady Bignor asked, "What made you come down so early, my dear? You'd have been better advised to burst on us in all your glory – though I'm thankful you didn't."

As she spoke she caught a watchful look on the other's face.

Cressida was listening intently, anxiously – for whose footsteps?

In a flash Cressida's old friend solved at least part of the enigma which had puzzled her. But though it was unfortunately only too natural for Cressida and Larry Wortle to have arranged to have a few minutes alone before dinner, why had Lizzie come down a full half-hour early? Had the girl, by some unlucky chance, discovered their assignation?

She put her hand on Cressida's arm.

"I want to say something to you."

"Say away, dearest! But don't forget I've got to undress and dress again."

"What I've got to say won't take a moment. It's only – *no poaching! Eh?*"

Cressida looked just a little hurt. "Now, do I ever poach?"

"I've never known you do anything else, you naughty girl. Sometimes I've suspected that it wasn't your fault – that you really couldn't help yourself!"

To that Cressida made no answer. Instead, she turned a searching, questioning look at the older woman. It was as if a mask had fallen off the lovely face, leaving it, if haggard, still most beautiful, and filled with tragic, mysterious implications – and confessions.

***

When Lady Bignor came down again to the drawing room, about five minutes past eight, she found her young friend wearing a simple, diaphanous black chiffon dress, in which Cressida looked so exquisitely pure, so enchantingly simple, so apparently unaware of her rare loveliness, that Major Mandeville felt the embers of his old heart stirred. So stirred, indeed, that in the billiard room, after the ladies had gone to bed, and Larry Wortle, out of immediate earshot, was knocking the balls about, he said to his old crony, George Slade, "'Pon my word! That girl would have been called a 'toast' a hundred years ago, eh, my boy? But none of you seem to be aware of it."

"Oh, yes, we are," replied the other with a queer smile. "We're all very well aware of it. Even more aware of it than the young lady herself."

5

Colonel Slade had spent the morning in taking a long walk, and now he was striding back through the village which lay at the foot of the overhanging cliff-like hill on which stood Millhanger House.

He wanted, as he had put it to himself more than once, during a rather wakeful night, to think things out.

The day after tomorrow would be Christmas Day, and he would be back "home," in his solitary cottage the evening of Boxing Day, with, as only company, his old batman and the latter's ill-tempered if efficient wife.

The five days he had spent at Millhanger House had made him realise the weight of both his age, and of his loneliness. He was in the mood which makes a man give unwilling assent to at least part of the old saying, "A bachelor lives like a king, and dies like a dog."

He, George Slade, had not lived like a king, but he did feel he was in some danger of dying like a dog.

There was, to his mind, no companionship in the world like Alice Bignor's companionship. Not that they always agreed, not that he invariably approved of all she said or did. But "his nonsense suited her nonsense," and always had done so, from the days when he had been an almost penniless subaltern in a light infantry regiment.

He could still recall, nay even partly recapture, now and again, the thrill with which he had awakened to the fact that the Alice Bowden whom he could vaguely remember in long clothes, had grown into the most delightful girl in the world – and that he was head-over-ears in love with her! So much in love, indeed, that her worldly-wise mother had whisked her away to Italy for the winter.

Then had come India for him, and, for her, a marriage which had only lasted six years. But they had remained in touch, through his close friendship with her only brother; and later, as Lizzie's guardian, he had had many opportunities of meeting her.

But it was the war which had brought about a strengthening of their loose, if lifelong, tie; and during his infrequent "leaves" he had fallen in love with her all over again. So it seemed inevitable that, after he had retired from the Service, he should have taken a little place, which included some rough shooting, within a few miles of Millhanger House.

Even so, of late years, he had never been thrown with Alice Bignor as intimately as he had happened to be during these last few days, and, as a result, he had made up his mind he would ask her to be his wife.

He was very poor, and in his eyes Lady Bignor seemed better off than she had ever been. But he was aware that she had received a generous yearly allowance for her niece, and that this allowance would now come to an end. Only yesterday she had spoken to him as if she was already thinking of selling Millhanger House, and her casual confidence had seemed to open out his way. It would have irked him to hang up his hat in his wife's hall. Still, he would have done it, had she so willed, for he loved her – loved her, as he was beginning to realise, more than even he had supposed to be still possible.

Hastening along through the village street, unconsciously quickening his steps so as to be with Alice Bignor the sooner, he told himself, with a grim smile, that perhaps it had been his proximity to Larry Wortle's violent absorption in Cressida Daryl, that made him feel as he felt now.

Watching those two – the experienced alluring Circe, and her foolish, reckless victim, swept off his feet for the first time in his life by the sudden fierce blossoming of passion – Colonel Slade had told himself, more than once, that were he the sort of damn' good-natured chap who delights in interfering with other people's business, he would have said a word of warning to that despicable, and yet in a way much to be pitied, young man.

Then would come the inner reminder that it is always unwise to thrust oneself into other people's business, coupled with the comforting reflection that Cressida Daryl would soon be far away, weaving her spells round some less susceptible swain.

As he passed the noble sixteenth century parish church of the tiny hamlet nestling in the fold of a still unspoilt stretch of Surrey downland, he became conscious, with a slight feeling of annoyance, that Mrs. Lancaster, the rector's wife, was bearing down on him.

Not that he disliked her. Indeed, he respected the quiet, intelligent woman who put up so gallant and unobtrusive a fight against what had become, since the war, bitter poverty. Even so, he had no wish to stop and talk to her just now.

But George Slade was always both courteous and kindly in manner to any woman, so he stayed his steps and greeted her pleasantly enough.

As she came close up to him, he saw, with a slight sensation of discomfiture, that she looked – flustered was the word that occurred to him. And that was the last word to be naturally associated with Mrs. Lancaster.

"I want to ask you a question, Colonel Slade."

"Not, I hope, an indiscreet question?"

"You may think it so, for it's about" – then with an effort she brought out, to his great surprise, the name— "Lizzie Bowden."

At once, inwardly, Lizzie's ex-guardian became sharply alert.

Was it possible that during the two hours he had been out this morning the girl had broken her engagement, and that already the news had reached the rectory? He knew that he would be glad, rather than sorry, if that were so.

But the next words uttered by Mrs. Lancaster undeceived him, as to the cause of her obvious agitation, for "I want to know if Lizzie Bowden is still engaged to Captain Wortle," she said firmly.

"Unless the engagement has been broken off since I left the house a couple of hours ago, she is certainly still engaged to him. But why d'you ask?"

"Because," she said slowly, "of something which happened yesterday."

Yesterday? What had happened yesterday? Then he recalled that the whole party had gone over to lunch at a neighbouring country house.

Larry Wortle had taken Lizzie, as in duty bound, in his two-seater, and, as a result, her cold, which had nearly gone, thanks to the care she had taken of herself for the last few days, was much worse again today.

Nothing else had occurred yesterday, that he could remember.

Instinctively lowering her voice, though they were standing quite close to one another on the deserted roadway, his companion continued: "My husband went into our church after tea, and, and..." – she waited for a long, uncomfortable moment, while he gazed at her, wondering what it was she was going to say— "he found Captain Wortle and Miss Daryl there together and behaving, I fear I must say, as lovers."

He tried to look as shocked and surprised as he knew she expected him to look.

"You don't think Mr. Lancaster can have been mistaken?" he asked.

There rose a spot of red on each of her pale cheeks.

"My husband is the kindest of men – also the most unobservant. Unlike me, he always gives everyone the benefit of the doubt. Yet what he saw made it quite clear to him that those two had deliberately gone into the church because they thought that they were in no danger of being caught. Or, if caught—"

She stopped again and he said "Yes?" interrogatively.

"—well, without ample warning of anyone's approach."

"Did they see the rector? Did he speak to them?" he asked, with some curiosity.

She shook her head. "He was wearing his indoor slippers, for, as you know, Colonel Slade, there's a door leading straight from the rectory into the church. Also, the two were completely absorbed in each other."

George Slade told himself that in the rector's place he would have remained mum. But aloud, he said, "And what do you and Mr. Lancaster think ought to be done?"

She answered without a moment's hesitation, "We think Captain Wortle ought not to be allowed to become poor little Lizzie's husband."

And then she asked a half-question, which had been in George Slade's mind many a time during the last few days: "What can have possessed Lady Bignor to have Cressida Daryl at Millhanger House just now? One would have thought she would have had more sense! I have always so disliked that girl. Even in the days when she was very young, and used to be here so much, there was always something heartless and sinister about her."

"I know what you mean," he said thoughtfully. "It's as if Cressida Daryl had no soul."

"She certainly behaves as if she had no conscience," observed Mrs. Lancaster sharply. Then: "Can't something be done, Colonel Slade?" she said earnestly.

He answered slowly, "Unfortunately Lizzie Bowden really cares for Captain Wortle. I wish to God she didn't. But she does."

"Would she go on caring, if she knew the way he's behaving now?"

He said in a low, musing tone, "I doubt if anything would ever make Lizzie believe a word against Larry Wortle. She's quite infatuated with him, and the date of their wedding was actually fixed yesterday. It's to be on the third of February – almost exactly five weeks from now."

He added ruefully, "It's a devilish difficult problem you've set me, Mrs. Lancaster."

"Perhaps I spoke too strongly just now," she answered. "The world has altered so much since I was a girl. I know that if my husband had behaved, when we were engaged, as Captain Wortle is behaving now, I—I—"

And then Colonel Slade burst into hearty laughter. He really couldn't help it. And his companion, having a sense of humour, laughed too.

But it was very seriously that she uttered her final words: "I'm sure that whatever you and Lady Bignor decide will be right."

Then they shook hands, and he hurried on, forgetful, now, of his own affairs, his mind entirely concentrated on the painful question of what he ought to do, or, rather, if he ought to do anything.

The problem was the more difficult because he had become more and more uncomfortably and anxiously aware, in the last few days, that Lizzie Bowden's feeling for Larry Wortle was very different from the average girl's way of being in love with a man whose offer of marriage she has accepted after a short acquaintance.

Lizzie, without doubt, already loved Wortle with all the passion and strength of her strong, if narrow, nature. Was it fortunate or unfortunate – so Lizzie's ex-guardian now asked himself – that owing, to a certain extent, to the accident of her cold, and her way of coddling herself, she rarely saw Cressida and Larry together, excepting when the whole party was present? But for that fact, she surely could not have remained what he believed her still to be, entirely unsuspicious.

As to Lady Bignor, Colonel Slade had wondered more than once whether she could be really aware of what was going on? Sometimes he thought yes, sometimes no. It was as if he and she had tacitly entered into a pact not to mention either Cressida Daryl or Larry Wortle, the one to the other.

But, as he came into Millhanger House, the door of the drawing room opened.

"Is that you, George? Will you come here for a minute?" And the voice which uttered those words was quite unlike Lady Bignor's fresh, eager voice. It was a fretful, anxious, almost ill-tempered voice.

He hurried towards her, with a word of apology for his muddy shoes.

Her face was flushed, and she looked, what she very seldom did look, disturbed and undecided.

"I've been longing for you to come in!" she exclaimed. "Where have you been?"

But she did not wait for him to answer before she added, in a lower, pleading voice, "I want you to do something for me, George."

He answered quietly, "You've only got to say what – and it's as good as done, Alice."

Her troubled face broke into a smile.

"I know that. But you won't find it easy to do what I want you to do."

He smiled back, "Out with it!"

"I want you to devise some way of keeping Larry Wortle either here, or of taking him over to your house, this afternoon. In fact, it doesn't matter to me where he is – as long as he's not at Birlings Place."

"I'll do my best," he began slowly, "but I can't force a grown-up man to do my bidding."

And then this dear woman, whom he loved with so unselfish a love, spoke to him, for the first time in her life, in a very disagreeable tone.

"What cowards men are! Surely you can manage a little thing like that to please me?"

As, surprised and hurt, he said nothing, she came close up to him.

"Don't look so cross, George – and forgive me for being so horrid—" her voice broke. "The truth is I'm miserable."

Taking her hand, he held it clasped in his, as she went on, "I'm horribly afraid that Lizzie, poor child, is beginning to get jealous. In fact, I'm quite sure she's beginning to suspect the idiotic way Cressida Daryl is carrying on with Larry Wortle."

"Idiotic? I call it devilish!" he said savagely.

"Well, whatever it is, Larry is much the worst of the two. It's amazing to me that Lizzie can like such a cad!"

"The girl has always been self-satisfied and vain," he said irritably. "But for that she couldn't have remained so blind."

Alice Bignor drew away her hand from that kind strong clasp.

"Really, George, you are a cynic. Would you expect a poor little girl who is only just engaged to suspect her lover of loving another woman, and at a moment's notice? Why, Cressida only arrived here five days ago. Larry Wortle must be mad."

"The young chap is mad, dangerously mad, for the moment."

"Then what's to be done?"

"Can't you make a strong, I mean a really strong, appeal to Miss Daryl?" he asked gravely.

Never, never had he, or would he, call Cressida by her Christian name, though again and again she had begged him, and oh, so prettily, to do so.

"I've tried, George, indeed, I have. But it was no good. She simply denies that there's anything to it. I do think that it's Larry's fault far more than hers. I really do. After all, he is the one who is engaged."

Colonel Slade could not forbear, kind as he was, and much as he cared for her, from carrying the war into the enemy's country.

"Why did you allow Cressida Daryl to come here just now?" he asked sternly.

Up flew the white flag.

"You can't blame me more than I blame myself," and again the tears came into the eyes George Slade thought still so beautiful.

"I don't blame you, Alice. I never do blame you," he said with some emotion. "I'm surprised, that's all. Cressida Daryl has always been a wrong 'un where men are concerned. Fond as you are of her, you must know that. As for Wortle, I've met some pretty low-down cads in my time, but I've never met such a—" then he deliberately used a word she had never heard from his lips— "swine, as that young chap is now proving himself to be."

"I suppose he's what Americans call 'a parlour lizard'?" and she smiled a wintry smile.

"It's gone deeper with him than that," he said grimly. "But there was a time when he could have pulled himself up – there always is."

"It wouldn't matter – I mean the engagement being broken off – if Lizzie didn't care. But oh! George, I'm afraid she does care, dreadfully."

"What makes you think she knows anything?" he asked uncomfortably. He was wondering again if anything had occurred in the two hours that he had been out, away from the house.

"I'm not sure that she knows whatever there is to know," she answered hesitatingly. "But I've a strong feeling that she suspects."

"Why d'you think that, Alice?"

He looked at her hard. "They've been precious careful, you know."

"I know they have – and yet, George? To my mind he's always giving himself away! Sometimes I feel quite sick when I see the three of them together."

"So do I," he answered sombrely.

"It's so difficult to say why one thinks a thing. But – well, though the child's really ill today, and though she's got a temperature, she was determined to get up and come down this morning. That was so unlike Lizzie, wasn't it?"

He nodded, gloomily; and she put her hand on his arm with a caressing touch.

"I wish you'd say a straight word to him, George?"

"I would – if I thought it would do any good. But unless I'm much mistaken, it would only make my future relations with him difficult, not to say unpleasant. Also, I'm sure he'd simply deny it – as you say she does."

"But what's to be done? Something must be done. Thanks to my having had to force poor Lizzie to stay in bed today, they spent the whole of this morning alone in the study together. Then, when Lord Danesborough sent a car over for Cressida, I overheard her telling Larry he was expected there this afternoon."

"That can be stopped at any rate," said Colonel Slade quickly. "I'll tell him what is, as a matter of fact, the simple truth, that the marriage settlement business must be discussed between us today; and I'll suggest taking him over to my place after lunch."

"Then he can come back and have tea with Lizzie," said Lady Bignor eagerly. "Thank you so very, very much, George! What should I do without you?"

"Get on very nicely by yourself, I'm afraid."

As she shook her head, he went on, "Well, that's settled, eh? In any case, I think I can assure you that I'll stop young Wortle's going off to Birlings Place this afternoon. That's what you want me to do, isn't it?" The word "dearest" nearly slipped out.

If there was going to be an upset, if Lizzie's engagement was going to be broken off, his poor dear Alice would be in no mood to think of anything but Lizzie. He told himself a little sadly that he had waited so long for her that it wouldn't hurt him to wait a little longer.

"How I wish Cressida would marry," said Lady Bignor suddenly. "Young Danesborough must be quite fond of her, or he wouldn't be always sending over for her."

"He may be fond of her; but I don't see him making her Lady Danesborough. I hear he's a shrewd young chap."

"He might go further and fare much worse, George," she cried defensively.

"D'you really think that marriage would alter Cressida Daryl?"

And he marvelled, not for the first time, at the denseness good women show, when the riddle of sex is put to them.

"I do, George! Cressida is very clever, and if she made a good marriage, she'd mind her p's and q's. It isn't as if she hadn't sown her wild oats!"

He said slowly, "Men and women aren't quite alike as to that, Alice."

And, hearing him make that observation, Alice Bignor wondered inwardly at the denseness of decent men where feminine human nature is concerned.

But all she said, lightly, was, "I think, as to that, God is as kind to women as He is to men, my dear George."

***

A few moments later Colonel Slade came across Larry Wortle in the hall.

"I'm sorry to hear that Lizzie's ill today," he observed, trying to speak pleasantly.

To that the young man made no answer; he looked sullen, and indeed far from well himself.

"As you're at a loose end, I'd be obliged if you'd go with me over to my house after lunch. I want to have a quiet talk with you. I heard from Mr. Coxe this morning concerning the final draft of Lizzie's marriage settlement. We might have a pow-wow about it, and come back here before tea."

Colonel Slade spoke with blunt decision. He felt for the moment as if he were back in the regiment, dealing with a difficult, ill-conditioned subaltern. A good dressing down, he told himself, would do this young chap all the good in the world.

"Thank you very much, sir. But I wonder if you could make it tomorrow, for I've promised to go to Birlings Place this afternoon?"

"I'm afraid you must telephone to say you can't keep your word. I've got to let Coxe know about the final draft of Lizzie's settlement by tomorrow morning."

There was a strained pause. Then Colonel Slade said quietly,

"Nothing can be done without Coxe; he's got all Lizzie's money matters in hand; and he's leaving England on Boxing Day for a month's holiday." He waited a moment, then, "As I think you know, she wishes to make a far more generous provision for you than is usual in such a case. Also there's the question of the sum which has been put aside for the purchase of a house. Coxe wanted me to talk it all over with you. But, if you like, we can of course postpone the whole discussion till the end of January. You and Lizzie may just as well be married in March as in February."

He looked straight into Larry Wortle's lowering face, and he saw, with bitter satisfaction, that his shot had gone home.

The young man crumpled up as, throwing back his head with a characteristic gesture, he exclaimed, "All right, sir. I'll telephone Birlings Place. It's very good of you to take so much trouble."

Lady Bignor, coming out of the drawing room, looked questioningly from the one to the other.

"We are going over to my house immediately after luncheon," said Colonel Slade quickly. "But we'll come back before tea – if we may?"

She turned conciliatingly to the young man.

"I expect that you'll like to have tea with Lizzie, Larry? She's not at all infectious. Besides, if she was, I'm sure you wouldn't mind!"

He muttered glum acquiescence, and his hostess went on,

"I'll send the car over to Birlings Place for Cressida. Perhaps I'll go myself, too. It's rather absurd that I've never even seen the new neighbour who's always entertaining someone belonging to my party."

She said the words quite good-humouredly, but, as she turned away, Larry Wortle threw her an inimical look.

She was a hateful woman! How could Cressida stand her, let alone like her, as she certainly did? He felt extremely angry, as well as intolerably disappointed; but he could not, he dared not, disregard the almost command of Lizzie's trustee.

He made himself, however, quite pleasant at lunch; so much so, indeed, that his hostess began, in her heart, to blame Cressida Daryl far more severely than she had yet done. She even told herself that, when not exposed to Cressida's beckoning charm, Larry Wortle was quite a well-mannered young man.

***

After seeing her two guests off in Colonel Slade's old Ford car, Lady Bignor went up to Lizzie's bedroom, happy in the thought that she would be bringing good news.

The girl lay propped up on pillows, trying to read. She looked both ill and wretched.

"I've just come up to see how you are getting on, my dear? George Slade has taken Larry off to his own house for the afternoon. He wants to make real friends with him, and there are one or two points about your marriage settlement which still have to be discussed. After they have had their talk, they'll come straight back, and Larry wants to come up here and have tea with you."

She saw Lizzie's face change; it was as if the sun had suddenly come out of a cloud.

"How lovely!"

The invalid clapped her hands like a happy child. Then she said wistfully, "But I don't want Larry to catch my cold, Aunt Alice."

"How about me, you naughty little girl? But Larry will run no risk of getting your cold – especially if you don't let him kiss you."

"Of course I won't."

Then she asked suddenly, "How long is Cressida Daryl going to stay here?"

"I said she could stay till after the New Year; but I believe she's leaving on the twenty-ninth. Has it ever occurred to you—"

"What?" asked Lizzie eagerly.

"— that Lord Danesborough must be very fond of Cressida? He's asked her over to Birlings Place every single day since she arrived here. She's there now. He sent for her before lunch, and I believe she's going on there from here."

"I expect she asked herself," observed Lizzie coldly. "She's always been like that."

6

THE NEXT DAY, THAT is on the morning of Christmas Eve, Lizzie felt very much better. Even so, she sent a message to say that, though she hoped to be down to lunch, she would stay in bed till then.

The little party, including Cressida, were already at breakfast when the message was given to Lady Bignor, and each of the four not only felt, but looked, relieved.

Colonel Slade had come to like young Wortle very much better, when he had had him under his own roof. All the more so that, as to the delicate question of the marriage settlement, the young man had been not only reasonable, but had spoken in a very proper way of the generous way in which he was being treated.

As for Larry, Larry had received the reward a good, or partially good, conscience generally brings with it.

Yesterday afternoon he had spent quite a pleasant, peaceful hour in Lizzie's firelit bedroom, and, in a way, he had liked holding her hot hand.

After all, it is sweet to be loved, especially when one is unhappy, and Larry Wortle was very unhappy just now. He was learning, and he was no docile scholar, that passion is often a synonym for pain.

Cressida, too, felt more settled and peaceful than usual this morning. She had at last made up her mind to go to Egypt this spring, and, if no miracle occurred to prevent it, to marry, there, her millionaire admirer.

She knew that, as his wife, she would be able to lead exactly the kind of existence which suited her, and in the only kind of society with whom she thought life worth living. This agreeable state of things would, naturally, be especially the case when she and her husband were temporarily parted – and she intended their temporary partings to be frequent, once he and she had settled down to what she considered normal married life.

Cressida had told her kind, generous friend of her decision, and the secret confidence had taken a load off Lady Bignor's heart.

She, also, felt easier this morning than she had been for several days. When she had gone in for a moment to see her niece on her way to bed last night, the girl had actually put her arms round her neck, and kissed her affectionately.

Lizzie's aunt had reminded herself then, and the reassuring belief had survived the night, that human tangles have a way of straightening themselves out, if you leave them alone, or only allow yourself, if you happen to be an intelligent woman, to give just a little gentle pull here and there.

***

In the middle of the morning Lizzie woke from a doze to see the winter sun shining, and to hear the sound of a car drawing up to the front door, on the other side of the house. Was it – could it be – Larry and Cressida going off together to Birlings Place? If so, they would certainly stay on to lunch, and for the afternoon.

Tears of angry disappointment rose to her eyes, and with a feeling of helpless exasperation she recalled what a selfish, hateful creature Cressida had shown herself to be – these last few days.

Cressida treated Millhanger House just as if it was an hotel, and she seemed to think that Larry Wortle had nothing better to do but to run after her, and obey her behests. Again and again she had made him drive her, in that horrid hired two-seater, not only to Birlings Place, but in and out of Guildford, as well.

It was very foolish of Aunt Alice to put up with such behaviour on the part of a visitor. She, Lizzie, would never have Cressida in her house, not even if Larry asked her to do so...

She got out of bed, and went over to a window, to see, a few moments later, that her suspicions had been baseless. It was Colonel Slade's ancient Ford car which was bumping down the steep garden drive, and by its owner's side sat Lady Bignor.

Then Cressida and Larry must be alone together downstairs?

There swept over the girl a sudden gust of jealous pain. Larry Wortle belonged to her, Lizzie Bowden. Though she, Lizzie, was ill, Cressida Daryl had no right to take up even a fraction of the time he ought to spend in answering the people who had written to congratulate him on his engagement.

Of course Larry might now be engaged in writing these duty letters, but somehow Lizzie didn't think this likely.

Why shouldn't she get up now, and go down and find Larry? Her temperature was normal; that proved she was really well again. Also, it was a beautiful, mild day – the sort of day that sometimes comes to happy England in the depths of winter, to show that spring will soon be here.

Why not ask Larry to take her out for a short walk before luncheon? Even Lizzie, today, thought that a little fresh air would do her good.

Though she felt weak and tottery, she dressed in feverish haste. After putting on her second-best short fur coat, for Lizzie was careful of her clothes, as she was of everything else, she jammed on one of her unbecoming country hats, and went slowly downstairs.

For a few moments she stood in the hall, but the house seemed unnaturally still. So after stepping aside to glance into the billiard room, she went on to the sunny drawing room, to find no one there.

That probably meant that the two who were now never out of her mind were together, out-of-doors, pacing up and down "the quarterdeck," as the one level path in the garden of Mill-hanger House was called.

Quietly Lizzie shut the drawing room door, crossed the empty hall, and opened the front door. It was certainly colder than she had expected to find it; but she was warmly clad.

Walking slowly, she started out and began skirting round the house on her way to the path where she expected to find Larry Wortle and Cressida Daryl.

And then, as she approached the window of the study – the apartment which in the summer she used as a sitting room, and which had lately been sacred to her and to her lover – an unpleasing possibility flashed into Lizzie's mind, and made her suddenly stay her steps.

Since the day following Cressida's arrival, she and Larry had never gone into the study. Her cold had been so bad that she had had to stay in bed to breakfast each morning, and no fire even had been lit there of late. She had heard Lady Bignor give the order for its discontinuance.

But if Cressida and Larry were still indoors, they must be in the study. That fact, if it was a fact, could easily be ascertained by her, and without their becoming aware of it.

The one window of the rather dark room formed a square bow, and through the panes of glass which composed the sides of the bow, any Peeping Tom could see into the study without being observed by its occupants.

So Lizzie's aunt had significantly reminded her, just after Lizzie had become engaged.

Now, rather to her surprise, the narrow glass panel to which she was now near was open a few inches from the bottom.

That was a bit of real luck!

She looked round; there was no gardener in sight; and, if there had been, she surely had every right to look into her own sitting room?

So, crouching down on the grass path, she gazed with eager eyes into the interior of the small, book-lined apartment.

For a few moments, blinded by the bright, if wintry, sun outside, she saw nothing. And then... then there arose a horrible physical commotion in all Lizzie Bowden's being; indeed, she had to grip the window ledge tightly, otherwise she would have fallen to the ground.

Larry Wortle, standing with his back to the now fireless grate, held Cressida in his arms. Her golden head was thrown back, and he was kissing her. . .

Now and again he would hold her away from him for a moment, murmuring, as he did so, "Dearest," "Angel," "Love," in a voice that the unhappy Lizzie had never heard, a voice broken with deep, ecstatic, emotion.

How long did she crouch down there, gazing at those two? It seemed to her an eternity, and indeed it may have been as long as two or three minutes.

At last, still crouching, and as if bent in agony, she moved back and sideways a few steps.

Then, closing her eyes, she straightened herself, and leant against the trellised wall of the house for a few moments.

Consciously she wondered how a human being could endure such torture of mind and spirit, and live.

Mercifully, she did at last turn faint – faint and sick, while, moving very slowly, she crept round on the grass path, and so back into the hall.

She waited there, still as if blind with pain, listening. But no sound came through the little lobby which led to the study, and so, at last, hardly knowing what she was doing, she went upstairs, and walked slowly, slowly, down the corridor leading to her bedroom.

Locking the door for the first time in her life, she flung off her coat and hat, and threw herself down on the unmade bed.

With her eyes still dry, she groaned aloud. What was she to do? What could she do?

Yet not for a moment did she even consider the possibility of giving up Larry Wortle. She felt in very truth as if he were already bone of her bone, and flesh of her flesh.

At last she turned and lay with her face crushed into the pillow, while, in a burning flood, came the acrid relief of tears.

***

An hour later, the unhappy girl heard Colonel Slade's old car puffing and whining up the carriage way. That must mean that it was close to lunchtime?

Slowly she rolled off her bed, and gazed in the mirror which stood on her dressing table. Her eyelids were swollen, and she looked very pale; also, as she noticed dully, undoubtedly less "nice" than usual, though not as "bad" as she had thought she would look.

Resolutely she took off her rough tweed skirt and jumper; and, after carefully bathing her face in cold water, and brushing her hair, she put on what she considered her smartest day frock. It was jade green in colour, with panels of embroidery which were supposed to impart, to quote the dressmaker's phraseology, a slendering effect. Then she went down to the drawing room.

No Cressida? No Larry? Only Colonel Slade and Lady Bignor.

Then the two must be still in the study – the fireless study where they had known no one would think of seeking for them.

Lizzie's heart contracted with a spasm of such anguished jealousy that she felt a sensation of physical, as well as mental, torment.

More than once, just as the luncheon bell rang, Larry had laughingly pleaded with her for "just one more kiss." That, no doubt, was what Larry was now pleading for to Cressida.

Her aunt exclaimed with concern at Lizzie's look of deadly illness and, for once, the girl tried to act.

"I did feel queer again this morning, Aunt Alice. But I'm better now," she murmured.

"I wonder if you ought to have come down?"

As Lady Bignor said the word "down," Lizzie's listening ears heard the door of the distant study open, and a moment later Cressida Daryl appeared alone, looking her usual calm, unruffled, nymph-like self.

After a while – it seemed a long, long time to Lizzie Bowden – Larry Wortle strolled in, too.

She threw him a swift glance. Then she averted her eyes. He appeared stern, preoccupied, haggard. Was it like that that men looked who loved?

After a moment of hesitation he came across to where Lizzie was sitting. He even sat down by her, and there came over his grave face an expression of sudden concern.

He took hold of her hand. "You look awfully bad, darling! Ought you to have come down?"

Twice she opened her mouth, but she found she could not speak. Still, she forced herself to smile at him.

"Your hand is so cold!" he exclaimed.

He had uttered the kind words in a very low voice, not wishing Cressida to hear.

"Is it? I look much worse than I feel," Lizzie whispered back.

And her tone was so gentle, and so much pleasanter than usual, that the young man was agreeably surprised.

Quickly he told himself that now, with others present, and the girl sitting by his side in an exceptionally amiable mood, would surely be a favourable moment to grasp a certain nettle of whose sting he felt perhaps foolishly afraid.

"Miss Daryl is going to Egypt the end of February, darling; and she wonders whether we'd mind her being on the same boat as we mean to go by?"

He still spoke in a low voice; but Cressida, standing by the fire warming her toes, heard what he said, and told herself he was a damned fool.

"I wouldn't be third in a honeymoon for the world!" she exclaimed, suddenly turning round.

But Larry Wortle went on, as if he had not heard the interruption.

"Our honeymoon will be practically over, won't it, Lizzie, by the time we leave for Egypt?"

The bell, a sweet tinkling bell, chimed in the hall, calling them to luncheon, and Lizzie got up from the chair on which she had been sitting.

Larry rose, too; but his eyes, full of sombre fire, were fixed on her pallid face, insistently demanding an answer.

"Of course our honeymoon will be over by then, and it will be very nice if you can manage to come with us," she said tonelessly, addressing, not Larry, but Cressida.

As she moved towards the door, her aunt again looked at her anxiously.

"Don't be cross with me, child – but I really do think you ought to go straight to bed again. You don't know how ill you look."

"I daresay you're right, Aunt Alice. I will go back to bed. And—and—" she stopped, feeling she could not go on.

"Yes, my dear?"

"I don't want any lunch. I'll have a cup of tea early," she muttered in a strangled voice.

Lady Bignor felt relieved, also a little moved, by the girl's submissiveness. Secretly she put down her niece's obviously suffering physical condition to indigestion, caused by the fact that Lizzie had insisted on being allowed to have a good dinner in bed last night.

She had felt so well, and she had been so happy after Larry's long stay in her room at teatime, that her usual robust appetite had come back, after three days of almost starvation.

"It would be so horrid if you had to be in bed on Christmas Day, child! Don't think of coming down again. Larry can come up and have his tea with you this afternoon, as he did yesterday."

***

Lizzie waited till the other four had gone into the dining room; then she crept out into the hall, and at the bottom of the staircase stood for a few moments quite still, listening.

The dining room door, which had a curtain over it, was not quite shut, and she heard her aunt say to the parlourmaid, "Miss Bowden won't have any lunch. She is going back to bed, and she will ring, later on, for a cup of tea."

Then the murmur of voices, happy voices, floated across the hall. Colonel Slade said something; Cressida laughed in answer; and there came a merry word from Lady Bignor. Not one of them, not even Aunt Alice, or kind George Slade, gave her a thought, and that though she was ill, and feeling miserable unto death.

She began walking upstairs. And, as she stepped on the broad treads of the staircase, she felt so dazed with angry pain that twice she stumbled heavily.

Cressida Daryl as travelling companion to Larry and herself during the last half of their honeymoon? The suggestion filled her with a sense of unendurable outrage. Yet, if Larry was set on Cressida being on the ship with them, how could she, Lizzie, prevent it?

Every fibre of her being refused to pick a serious quarrel with the man she loved, and whom she still felt to be, in a curiously intimate sense, part of herself.

Though she could not have put it into words, the unhappy Lizzie Bowden felt as many a mediæval woman must have felt concerning a renegade lover – that Larry had been bewitched out of his real self; that he had been ensnared, cajoled into infidelity.

Frightful as was Larry's treachery to herself, she yet could find excuses for him – though none, none for his temptress.

Two nights ago, after her successful onslaught on what, to herself, she called Cressida's indecent costume, she had remained oddly wakeful. And during the hours she had tossed about, this way and that, between what had seemed to her shivering body burning sheets, she had felt convulsed with vaguely jealous thoughts.

But the morning had brought back her usual self-satisfied feeling of security; and the certainty that Larry loved her – only her. He might flirt a little with Cressida – all men, except George Slade, seemed as if they couldn't help doing that – but in his heart Larry must despise her, utterly. Men always despise girls who run after them. Everyone knows that.

But now Lizzie knew that she had been a fool, lulled by – was it vanity? – into false security. There sprang to her mind two famous lines she had read many a time, with an utter lack of understanding, as a schoolgirl,

"Who cried – `La belle Dame sans Merci'Hath thee in thrall!"

Cressida, wicked heartless Cressida, had poor Larry in thrall. How strange that she, Lizzie, had not suspected it yesterday, and the day before yesterday, and the day even before that.

At last she reached the top of the staircase, and began walking along the broad corridor which ran down the visitors' wing of charming Millhanger House.

Slowly she dragged herself along, her mind in a maze of mortal pain, aye, and of what is so much more intolerable than pain, her body in the throes of physical jealousy.

Again and again she asked herself what she could do to rescue her lover? But, try as she might, she could think of no way out. No way, that is, by which she could hope to expel, forever, Cressida from her own and Larry's life.

This dreadful certainty as regarded the future was the more unendurable because she realised, what a fundamentally stupid person would not have done, that what was death – and far, far more than death – to her, Lizzie Bowden, and even to haggard, enthralled Larry Wortle, was only sport to Cressida Daryl.

The girl knew with that intuitive knowledge which is the most certain knowledge of all, that Cressida did not love Larry. Cressida only loved herself, while welcoming, with a kind of dainty greediness, the sensual enjoyment which was to her the concomitant of the passion she found so easy to arouse in men.

So much the unhappy Lizzie dimly apprehended, while groping her way, for the first time in her life, among the hidden, earthy roots of our poor human nature.

Now and again she stopped in her slow progress, and stared down to her left, into the courtyard down one side of which ran the visitors' wing.

The thought of undressing and of lying down again on that bed on which she had flung herself an hour ago was insufferable, and yet she would have to do so, in a few moments.

Slowly, slowly she moved on, as in a waking trance, until, at last, she stayed her steps opposite the half-open door of Cressida Daryl's bedroom.

7

THE BLUE ROOM, AS it was called, was the principal guest-chamber of Millhanger House; and had there been an older woman visitor, or a married couple, staying here for Christmas, Cressida would have been elsewhere, in a bedroom situated in the other wing, near Lady Bignor's own apartments.

But as there was no other woman visitor, and as Cressida was her special pet, Lady Bignor had arranged that, "for once," as she had herself expressed it when giving her orders to her trusted upper housemaid, "Miss Daryl should be in the blue room, and so thoroughly comfortable."

Feeling slightly ashamed of what she was doing, Lizzie, after she had stood for a few moments just outside the blue room, pushed the door a little wider open, and looked furtively into the delightful bedchamber.

At once she noticed that a big fire was burning away in the high grate, and the sight of that fire, burning to waste, exasperated her.

Every woman, however generous, has her pet economies. Though there was no central heating above the ground floor of her country house, Lady Bignor did not allow either her own bedroom fire, or that of her niece, to be lit before, say, teatime, even in very cold weather, unless, of course, either of them happened to be ill.

But Cressida Daryl always airily disregarded any rule of any house which interfered with her personal comfort, and when on a winter visit she had the fire lit in her bedroom the moment she was called in the morning.

The fire in the blue room had evidently been made up quite a short time ago, so none of the maids would have any reason for coming to this part of the house till after tea. And, following some obscure impulse, born of her present absorption in Cressida's vivid, and to her now hateful, personality, Lizzie suddenly walked right through the door into the large warm room.

For a moment the interloper stood close to the door, and tears rose to her aching eyes.

She had become resentfully aware of a delicate fragrance – that of the costly, unusual scent Cressida always used.

She, Lizzie, had always thought the use of scent common and unladylike; now she wondered, forlornly, if Larry liked its use by a woman.

Standing there, in the beautiful room where everything seemed to speak of her rival's physical charm and beckoning allurement, there came over Lizzie Bowden a sensation of despair, of such hopeless agony as she had not known could endure, in that secret world of inner thought and feeling in which every human being dwells solitary.

Her heart called out despairingly, "Larry – Larry – Larry." And suddenly, as if his wraith had been conjured up by that voiceless cry, the man Lizzie loved with such a fierce, if inarticulate, passion, seemed to be here, looking at her with cruel, mocking, alien eyes.

So intensely real was this feeling of her lover's physical presence, though reason told her that he was downstairs in the dining room, looking at Cressida, talking to Cressida, thinking of Cressida – that it amounted, almost, to an hallucination.

She covered her face with her hands. Was it because she was in a place where everything spoke, even smelt, of Cressida Daryl, that Larry Wortle seemed to be here too? The thought that this might be so brought with it such a sense of humiliation, as well as pain, that she gave a stifled cry.

Closing the door quietly, she went up to the blue silk-canopied bed, on which, carefully arranged on an embroidered Jacobean coverlet, already lay the things into which Cressida would change this evening. The maids were going to a junketing this afternoon, in the village hall. That was why the frock and the undergarments had been laid out so early.

How lovely they were, like part of a fairy's trousseau! And by them was spread out a lemon-coloured chiffon frock which its owner had not yet worn at Millhanger House.

As she gazed at the evening frock lying there, Lizzie remembered that she, herself, had decided to wear a dress of just that tint tonight. But now, with wits unnaturally sharpened, she told herself that only a girl dowered with Cressida's pale gold hair, and camellia-petal like skin, could look to advantage in so bright and delicate a colour.

She moved away, at last, from the side of the bed; and, while wandering aimlessly across the large room, she saw that, standing on the dressing table, were two medicine bottles and a medicine glass.

The larger bottle was almost empty; indeed, it obviously contained just one last dose of dark, almost black, liquid, which Lizzie knew to be Cressida's favourite "dope." It was the only stuff, or so Cressida had said more than once in Lizzie's hearing, which insured a perfect night's sleep with no after ill effects.

Lizzie took up the bottle, and then she doted with tepid interest that the prescription, which was printed on it in French, revealed the fact that it contained minute quantities of chloral and of strychnine, in addition to the staple, safe narcotic which formed its principal ingredient.

Cressida Daryl lived too fast; she made no secret of it; indeed, she was given to boasting that she was burning, not rusting, herself out.

Then, idly, Lizzie took up the other, smaller, bottle from the glass-covered surface of the dressing table.

The second bottle, of which the top formed a dropper, was about half full of a colourless liquid. It had pasted on its side a blue label on which was printed the one word "Strychnine," while on a white label was the name "Jean Robert," the word "Pharmacie," and an address in the Rue Saint Honoré.

Lizzie recalled the sound of Cressida's gay, lilting, voice, as it had sounded two or three days ago, when the rector and Mrs. Lancaster had come to tea. Smiling at Mr. Lancaster, who had a poor heart, she had asked,

"What's your binge? Mine's strychnine! I always get a provision of it when I'm in Paris, as it's much stronger than the stuff they sell here. Two or three drops make me feel as fit as a fiddle for quite a long time!"

Standing there, still with the bottle of that dangerous "binge" in her red, cold hand, Lizzie could almost feel the vibrations of Cressida's peculiar intonation as she had asked the rector that probing question in a light, roguish tone.

And she remembered Mr. Lancaster's answer. He had observed that strychnine was poison; a deadly poison, for all it looked like water, and so should be taken with due care and discretion.

Recalling those words, now, the girl gazed at the colourless liquid with a queer sensation of repulsion and attraction.

Once more she took up the larger bottle, and again she read, with far more attention than she had done the first time, the prescription printed in French.

There was strychnine in this black dope too – but only a tiny amount of it.

Lizzie put down the bottle by the medicine glass. Then, moving over to the fireplace, for she felt cold and shivery, she stood for quite a long time staring down at the leaping flames, while strange secret thoughts, vague possibilities, and definite hopes and fears, flashed through her brain – a brain now inflamed with a passionate sense of wrong.

At last she went over to the bedroom door and, opening it, she listened.

The house was very still, though from what seemed just now infinitely far away, downstairs, there came the murmur of cheerful voices floating out of the dining room.

Taking what she knew was a risk, though a very small risk, of being discovered to have done rather a curious thing, she locked the door.

Walking quickly back to where the two medicine bottles stood on the dressing table, she lifted up the larger, now nearly empty, bottle, took out the cork, and, with a steady hand, poured out half of the one large dose which was there, into the little medicine glass.

With the medicine glass in her hand she almost ran across to the fireplace, and threw the dark mixture it contained on to the glowing coals.

Having done that she returned to the dressing table, and waited a moment, as if lost in thought. Yet she was vividly, fiercely, alive to what she had done, and was about to do.

Mechanically she replaced the medicine glass where it had stood before, and, as she did so, she suddenly perceived the reflection of her face in the looking glass.

That she should be very pale, that she should be looking ill, was natural enough. But she saw something else in that carved Italian mirror. For the first time, in her grown-up life, Lizzie Bowden saw herself as she appeared to the eyes of those about her – that is, worse than ugly, plain. Plain and uninteresting.

Yet, whatever she might look to the indifferent, she reminded herself piteously that Larry Wortle, the only human being in her world who really mattered, had fallen in love with her at first sight. She couldn't doubt that – for he had told her so himself, speaking with great earnestness, when he had asked her to be his wife.

And Larry's love had grown as hers had done, during those happy, happy early days of her engagement, when only her aunt and Colonel Slade had known how matters stood between them. Were Cressida's magic wiles withdrawn, Larry would certainly return to her, his only love.

And the thought of Larry, while she was staring at the reflection of her pale, swollen face and red-rimmed eyes, brought back, oh, so poignantly, the wonderful moment when they had kissed for the first time, and – what she had seen, what she had heard, when peering into the study.

With a quick, decided movement, she took up the bottle containing what even she knew to be death in being. And, unscrewing the glass top which also formed a dropper, she poured the colourless, water-like strychnine into the larger bottle, till she had made up and, indeed, more than made up, the full dose that had been there.

Would Cressida notice that the last dose of her dark dope was lighter than usual? Almost certainly not.

After she had put the two bottles back exactly where she had first seen them standing, her eyes became focussed, with a pang of dismay, on the soiled medicine glass. How could she have been so stupid, so careless?

Taking up the small measured glass with a hand that trembled for the first time, she went across to the washstand, and, turning it over, she plunged it again and again into the full water-jug. When it was quite clean, she carefully wiped it dry, and polished it with her handkerchief.

Then, not till then, was she seized with a sense of panic.

Rushing across the large bedroom, she unlocked the door, opened it, and began slipping through it, intending to leave the door ajar, exactly as she had found it.

But, as she emerged into the corridor, to her surprise and discomfiture she saw Colonel Slade coming out of his bedroom next door.

What could have made him come up just now? How long had he been in his room? Could he have passed by while she was in the act of locking the door of Cressida's room?

She would never know the answers to these wordless, fright-ened questions, for she had been far too absorbed in herself, in her agonised thoughts, and in the task she had set herself, to have heard the slight sounds made by his steady footsteps in the carpeted corridor.

One of her frightened, wordless questions was soon an-swered, for, when close to her, "Lizzie!" he exclaimed, "I thought you'd gone straight up to bed?"

As she said nothing, he went on kindly: "You look very ill, my dear girl! Why not get old McLeod to come and have a look at you again?"

She shook her head, and answered by another question, "Is luncheon over, Uncle George?"

He gazed at her, surprised. "Oh no! We're not half through yet. I came up to get my new diary; your aunt wants to know when Easter falls next year."

Then she had only been a few minutes in the blue room? Looking back, it seemed æons of time.

They passed each other, and Lizzie slowly, reluctantly, went into her bedroom.

Though the room had been made, the fire had been allowed to go out, and she felt a touch of angry resentment at the fact.

Why was it that the servants all liked Cressida, and were eager to make her comfortable, but took no thought for one who was, after all, the young lady of the house?

She lay down on her bed, and put her burning cheek on the cool pillow. While feeling subconsciously terrified of the awful thing she had done, her mind became obsessed anew by what she had seen when gazing into the study. And many little incidents which had occurred in the last five days, and which surely should have awakened her suspicions, came back to her.

Amongst other things, she now recalled, with a feeling of painful indignation, a glance her aunt had cast on Cressida the very first evening. It had been a look of reproof, and yet, yes, an indulgent look. She, Lizzie, now realised that that glance of indulgent reproof had been evoked by the way Cressida had, even then, been trying to lure Larry away from the others.

Cressida had suggested – how clearly it all came back to Lizzie now! – that she and Captain Wortle should go out and see if there was any chance of snow. True, Aunt Alice had put a stopper on that suggestion; but she had not been disgusted, as she should have been at such forward behaviour. She had only been amused...

Lizzie Bowden told herself, now, what most of us live to tell ourselves, at some time or other of our lives – that is, how unfeeling, and how heartless, even kind and good people can be, about a matter which, if of dreadful moment to another, does not directly concern themselves.

Just after the clock in the hall had chimed half-past two, she heard, as she so often did hear, when in her bedroom, a car skidding down the steep drive.

Though she knew quite well, by the sound, that it was the two-seater Larry had hired in the village, she felt she must make sure. So, leaping from her bed, she rushed to the window.

Yes, of course it was they, Larry and Cressida, going off together. And that though Cressida, in the old days, never, if she could help it, entered an open car.

Lizzie waited, standing shivering by the window, though she was fully clothed, till the car, now little more than a flying speck, reappeared on the flat road which wound ribbon-wise across the valley below. Then, slowly, she went and lay down again on her bed, feeling spent with misery.

8

WHEN LIZZIE BOWDEN AWOKE it was late in the afternoon, and, as consciousness came back, she wondered for a moment if she had dreamt all that had happened in the blue room.

But that moment of doubt did not endure, and she recalled with a feeling of startled wonder and horror the perilous thing – perilous to herself, perilous to Cressida – that she had done. Yet she was curiously ignorant as to the possible, or probable, consequences of her act. In happier days Lizzie would have considered an interest in such a subject as poison, and its effects on the human body, as morbid, even indelicate.

Sitting up, she pressed her right hand on her eyes. Her eyes, her head, every bit of her, was aching.

Swinging her body round, she slipped off her bed. Then she went across to the door and, opening it, stood feeling uncertain what to do.

The lights had not yet been turned on in the corridor. That looked as if the maids had not yet returned from their Christmas Eve junketings. No doubt Colonel Slade and Lady Bignor, following Larry's and Cressida's example, had gone out driving too.

As Lizzie stood there, in the darkness, half in and half out of her bedroom door, she told herself, with a dull sense of shame, that she had been mad – mad when she had done that crazy thing.

Why, *if anything had happened*, she, Lizzie Bowden, would have been a murderess.

There came over her a startling impulse to laugh and cry – cry and laugh, at the astounding, absurd, incredible idea. But, six years ago, when she was at school, she had had what she had heard those about her call "a fit of hysterics," and she had never forgotten the feelings of humiliation and of shame which had followed.

Besides, this was no laughing matter. She must go now, at once, into the blue room. Once there, she must lock the door, empty the bottle of French dope into the fire, and hide the empty bottle till she could throw it away, out-of-doors.

In little things, Cressida Daryl was easy-going and good-natured. When she missed the bottle, she would naturally suppose it to have been broken by the under-housemaid, who had been afraid to tell, and ten to one she would say nothing about it.

After listening for a few moments to hear if anyone was coming up the back stairs, Lizzie stepped into the corridor, and opened the door of the blue room.

As she passed through it she was again assailed, enveloped, by the peculiar, fragrant perfume the present occupant of the room always used. And then, with a terrible acuity of vision, there rose before her in the firelit room cruel, wanton Cressida, and enslaved, false-hearted Larry – as she had seen them this morning.

Cressida's golden head was tipped back, and Larry, bending over her, was holding her to his heart, and kissing her. Now and again he would stop and gaze at her, filling his heart, his senses anew, with her loveliness. "Angel". . . "Dearest". . . "Love."

It was as if she, Lizzie Bowden, was once more playing eavesdropper as she had done this morning, in the wintry sunshine, excepting that now, thank God, it was dark.

All thought of undoing what she had done became obliterated. She left the blue room, shutting the door behind her, and, a moment later, her chance of undoing what she had done, at any rate for the present, was gone.

As she was retreating into her own room, the lights in the corridor were suddenly turned on, and she saw the kitchen maid, the only servant who had stayed at home this afternoon, emerge from the back staircase hard by, and go quickly into Cressida's bedroom.

There followed the sound of the lifting up of the coal scuttle, the shooting out of a generous measure of coal, and the drawing down of the blinds.

The young woman came out at last and, seeing Lizzie standing at her bedroom door: "Why, you did startle me, miss!" she exclaimed.

"I should like you to light my fire again, Jane."

The other asked doubtfully, "Before six, miss?"

"Yes, now," replied Lizzie firmly.

She told herself, with a sore feeling, that even when she hadn't a cold she had quite as much right to a fire, nay more right, than had any visitor. That if only because she had agreed to go on giving Lady Bignor the twelve hundred a year her aunt had been allowed by the trustees before she came of age.

Till today Lizzie had never thought of the matter with regard to herself and her personal comfort, but now she remembered it with a sudden surge of indignation.

She passed the young maid quickly, and ran downstairs into the drawing room. There she found Lady Bignor alone, sitting near the fire, reading.

"Aunt Alice!" she exclaimed. "I feel all right now, so I've come down. My fire was out when I went upstairs before lunch, and I've said it's be lit again, at once."

There was an angry challenge in her tone, but the other, who was full of anxious, troubled thoughts, remained unaware of the unpleasant edge in the familiar voice.

Lady Bignor put down her book, and looked round at her niece.

"You did quite right, my dear. Of course your fire ought to have been kept up. Indeed, it's so very cold just now, that I think you and I might each start our fires in the morning. I want you to keep well, child, during the next few weeks."

The voice in which these words were uttered was very kind; softer, too, than usual.

There came a choking sensation in the unhappy girl's throat. Why, oh why, had Aunt Alice allowed Cressida Daryl to come here just now? There came back to her – absurd and piteous recollection – the old tag, "Evil is wrought by want of thought, and not by want of heart."

Lady Bignor got up, and began moving restlessly about the room.

There was something she wished to say to her niece, which indeed she thought it her duty to say, and she did not quite know how to set about it.

At last she came close up to where Lizzie was still standing doing nothing, as was her way – a way which inwardly irritated her active-minded aunt.

"I'm sorry Cressida won't come with me to Monte Carlo," she observed.

As Lizzie said nothing in answer to that, she went on, a little nervously, "I don't think much of her notion of travelling with you and Larry to Egypt. I'm all for modern ways; but I do think that, on a honeymoon, two's still company and three is none."

Twice Lizzie opened her mouth, and twice she shut it again. Then she said slowly, "We shan't be starting for Egypt at once, Aunt Alice. We're to be at Rotherham Castle for ten days, and, I suppose, for a little while after that in London."

"Even so, there seems to me no reason in the world why Cressida should become your travelling companion," said Lady Bignor decidedly. "She can easily get hold of someone else who is going to Egypt about the same time, and I intend to tell her so."

"But please don't let Cressida think that I should mind, Aunt Alice – because I shouldn't."

There was a defiant note in the girl's voice, and Lady Bignor exclaimed, "Sit down, my dear. We're not often alone just now, and I want to say something to you."

Walking across to the door which Lizzie had left open, she shut it deliberately. Then she came back to where Lizzie had just sat down, unwillingly, on the edge of a high chair, and gazed anxiously into the sullen, flushed face.

Placing herself in an armchair close to her niece, she said firmly: "I want you to give me your whole attention, my dear."

Lizzie made no answer to that. Her thoughts were far away. She was visualising Larry and Cressida as she believed they must be now, seated very close to one another in that narrow little hireling.

And then, with a touch of deliberate self-torture, she caused to start into life another vision of those two. Larry had stopped the car on a dark, lonely, stretch of road, and he was kissing Cressida with that exultant, hungry, ecstatic look in his eyes which had been there this morning. "Love". . . "Dearest" . . . "Angel." . . . Lizzie could almost hear the words uttered – between their clinging, impassioned kisses – in the only voice she loved, or would ever love, in the world.

"Listen to me, Lizzie!"

With an inward start the girl came back to what was happening, here and now, in the drawing room of Millhanger House.

"Yes, Aunt Alice?"

"As I think you know, I don't believe in interfering in other folks' concerns; and I believe that young people ought to manage their own affairs."

She waited a moment. "You've often heard me say so, haven't you, child?"

Lizzie looked at her aunt; she wanted to say "yes," but even that little word stuck in her throat.

"Still, there's one thing more I should like to say to you, and then for ever hold my peace," went on Lady Bignor quickly.

Again Lizzie looked at her aunt dumbly.

"One of the facts I've learnt in my life is that a woman's a fool, however attractive she may think herself, and however much her husband may be in love with her, who deliberately throws him with an attractive—" she sought for the right word, but could only find a very old-fashioned noun to express what she meant to convey. That noun was "flirt."

Again she waited a moment. Lizzie (but of course that was Lizzie's way) was not making it easy for her.

All the same, she went on, in a lighter tone, "Sometimes, of course, it can't be helped; and I admit there's nothing a man hates like a jealous wife."

Lizzie, still dumb, was gazing at her with dull, lack-lustre, eyes. Lady Bignor told herself that the girl evidently hadn't understood the gist of the advice which had just been tendered her.

What a fool, as regarded anything to do with human nature, Lizzie was, to be sure; and how amazing that she should still be so blind!

Still, she, Alice Bignor, was bound to do her duty by her poor, vain, pig-headed little niece. So she forced herself to conclude her admonition with the very plain words, "Your Larry is a most attractive young man. In my opinion, you will have to keep your weather eye open where he's concerned, even after you and he are married."

To this well-meant further piece of advice Lizzie again made no answer. She felt not only horribly humiliated, but perilously near to tears.

Giving her a quick, anxious glance, Lady Bignor exclaimed, "You still look very ill, my dear! Why don't you lie down here, where it's nice and warm? I think some of the maids will soon be back, and I'm having tea taken up to my sitting room today. I'll send you down a cup."

But after her aunt had left her, though she got up from the uncomfortable chair on which she had been sitting bolt upright, and though she obediently put her feet up on the deep, roomy sofa, Lizzie Bowden could not rest.

Nice and warm here? Why, she felt deadly cold, as she lay listening . . . listening . . . listening. . .

A cup of tea was brought to her at five o'clock, and after that she sat up, and tried to read the book her aunt had put down. But the words danced before her eyes, making nonsense of each other, for she was still listening.

Two hours later, just before the dressing bell chimed, Larry Wortle and Cressida Daryl came back from what must have been an exceptionally long drive, and that even if they had broken it at some hospitable house for tea.

Lizzie, from the drawing room, heard her aunt running downstairs into the hall as the two-seater drew up at the front door. And then came Cressida's voice, raised rather more than usual,

"There was nothing to be anxious about, Aunt Alice. We went rather further than we meant to, that's all – and we had quite a good tea, in a nice little cottage, and the woman made us some hot buttered toast. But I'm tired now, fearfully tired!"

"Hadn't you better have dinner in bed, Cressida?"

Lady Bignor seldom spoke in so cold a tone to anyone as she did now, to her pet.

Lizzie heard the quick answer. "Oh, no! I shouldn't care to do that. A hot bath will soon bring me to life again. I'd far rather come down to dinner."

As for Larry Wortle, he spoke not at all, or, if he did, the girl who loved him, and who was to be his wife, did not hear the voice which at this moment she almost felt she hated.

She had forgotten, during those agonised hours of waiting, of listening, for her lover's return, what she had done in the blue room. Everything in her life, past, present, and future, had gone out of focus excepting Larry, and her own relation to Larry.

9

WHEN, HALF AN HOUR later, the party of five were gathered together in the drawing room, Cressida Daryl looked even more delicately lovely than usual.

She had taken special pains with her clever make up, and she had also coaxed Lady Bignor's maid, Cleary, to wave, for the second time that day, her pale gold shingled hair.

Colonel Slade, glancing across at her, reserved, unfairly enough, all his contempt, and most of his disapproval, for Larry Wortle. Yet the young man, so the older man told himself, did not look like a happy lover. Though outwardly the same, Larry, in his eyes, appeared oddly unlike himself tonight. It was as if he were in a sombre dream, withdrawn from everything and everybody about him.

As for the girl to whom he was, after all, still engaged, she simply looked, in her guardian's eyes, more insignificant and unattractive than usual, as well as far too ill to have come down to dinner.

Perhaps because two of the little party of five had such a right to feel tired, a heavy silence reigned for a while in the drawing room. Even the lively hostess felt there was nothing to say.

Cressida advanced, at last, as if instinctively, to the fire; and a moment later, Larry, as if moving in answer to something outside himself, slowly, yet deliberately, followed her there.

It was as if that movement in the room broke the spell, for Lady Bignor began talking eagerly, animatedly, to Colonel Slade of an incident connected with their distant youth.

It was a comfort to her to forget, even if only for a few moments, the uncomfortable present.

At last the dinner bell tinkled, and they all streamed across the hall into the dining room, now gaily decorated with holly and mistletoe.

A lonely stranger, looking in on this party of people sitting down to their Christmas Eve dinner, would have thought them a cheery gathering of happy, prosperous folk, each and all greatly to be envied by the disinherited of the earth. And it was true that three, out of the five there, did begin to feel very much more at ease than they had felt a few minutes ago.

Colonel Slade's mind went back, skipping the odious interlude in the drawing room, to the delightful time he had spent this afternoon with Alice Bignor, in her charming cosy sitting room upstairs.

After they had had tea, she had made him go and fetch his pipe, and they had had a long intimate talk over the days of their youth. They had discussed some of the men and women, good and bad, they had both known, passing now kind, now hard, judgments, as only really close friends do, concerning those who have long passed out of their lives.

He had felt very happy during that long intimate talk, and he had ventured to hope that she, his dear, dear Alice, had felt happy too.

That Colonel Slade was justified in that hope would have been apparent, now, to anyone less modest than himself.

Many years ago, when she was at odds with fate, Lady Bignor had been given one of those often futile little volumes containing ill-chosen quotations from great writers. One quotation, from George Herbert, had moved her heart. It ran, "There is an hour wherein a man may be happy all his life, can he but find it." Tonight she felt that she, though a woman, had found that hour. So why make herself anxious, and even unhappy, over the affairs of two selfish young people who, no doubt, knew perfectly well how to look after themselves?

Cressida Daryl always "played up," even when in a very small company of people. That was one of the agreeable attributes that made her so welcome, everywhere, as a visitor.

She was tired tonight, very, very tired. But after she had drunk half a glass of champagne, and eaten her cupful of hot turtle soup, she began telling, with a good deal of humorous detail, the inner story of a sensational libel case which had aroused a great deal of gossip. In spite of themselves, both Colonel Slade and Lady Bignor laughed heartily at her malicious, witty comments.

Also, though Cressida was tired, she none the less felt inwardly strung up, and even pleasantly excited, this evening; for something had happened during that long, fatiguing motor drive, which had thrilled and stimulated her jaded senses.

Larry Wortle had treated her – the right phrase – to what, looking back, she described to herself as a marvellous scene of passion. He had threatened, implored, and even burst into a storm of hard, difficult sobs, while explaining that now it had come to this with him – he could not, would not, face life without her.

When she had uttered, startled into sincerity for once, the one questioning word "Lizzie?" he had answered, desperately, that Lizzie had nothing to do with what he was saying and feeling now. Lizzie would never know – so the man for whom Lizzie felt so fierce and possessive a passion had confidently declared – of his and Cressida's secret, instinctive love for one another.

And when, still cool, though, as far as such a feeling could exist in her heart, touched by his agony, she had shaken her head – he had declared that if it was only Lizzie that stood in the way, he would throw over Lizzie.

But she, Cressida, had soon proved to him that to break his engagement would indeed be folly, and worse than folly! After all, it was money – no matter whose money – that made their world, his and her world, go round. And to that bit of unanswerable logic, the wretched Larry had found nothing to reply.

But his wild words of pleading, even his naïf belief that his absorption in herself would endure forever, had so far moved Cressida that she had been, perhaps unwisely, "kinder" than ever before. But, far from slaking his thirst, all she had dared to give only increased what she had begun to feel was Larry's danger-fraught frenzy.

Even so, how she had enjoyed, how thrilled she had been during the violent scene which had been torture to her companion.

It was simply amusing, now, to remember that she had felt, for a moment, really frightened, when suddenly he had stopped the car again in a cart track cutting through a lovely stretch of wintry woodland, to plead, with blazing eyes and in desperate accents, for a suicide pact between them.

In a queer, subtle way, the memory of those sunken, blazing eyes, and fevered, passion-laden words, gave Cressida an intense sensation of gratified – vanity were an unkind word; rather was it triumph, that she could arouse such primeval emotions in one as super-civilised as was the man now sitting opposite to her at Lady Bignor's black marble dining table.

As for Lizzie Bowden, to her Cressida Daryl gave no thought at all, save as the moneyed vehicle who would make easy innumerable future pleasures and intimate satisfactions.

Lizzie, after all, would get all that was possible – and a great deal more than she deserved.

Tonight the engaged couple were, as always, seated side by side, and now and again they exchanged a word or two.

But Larry Wortle, during the whole of the meal, went on being curiously abstracted. So much so indeed that both Lady Bignor and Colonel Slade observed his unusual withdrawal into himself. It was as if his thoughts were far away from the pleasant cheerful-looking scene. He ate, he drank, as if he were an automaton, and he avoided, perhaps a thought ostentatiously, either looking at, or speaking to, his amusing, witty, *vis-à-vis*.

Not one of them there – not even Cressida, with all her knowledge of love-stricken men, not even Lizzie, whose thoughts were wholly of Larry, and only of Larry – guessed that under that abstracted manner his mind was hard at work.

While he sat there, silent, eating and drinking like an automaton, Larry Wortle was racking his weary, excited brain to invent some excuse by the help of which he could leave Millhanger House on Boxing Day, in order to stay at, or near, Birlings Place.

Cressida Daryl had suddenly arranged by telephone to go on there the day after tomorrow, and, to himself, it admitted of no doubt that, by hook or by crook, he must go too. But the question was – how?

To offend Lizzie and Lady Bignor would be mere short-sighted folly; Cressida, this afternoon, had made that absolutely clear. And as his love, his darling love, had laid her commands on him to avoid "trouble" at all costs, he, her slave, must surely obey.

During those breathless days which had revealed to Larry Wortle a hitherto unsuspected world of mingled ecstasy and frustrate passion, he had only really felt alive when alone with Cressida Daryl. What short time he had been compelled to spend with Lizzie Bowden – a time mercifully shortened by the fact that she was one of those unfortunate people who are made really ill by a cold – seemed a throw-back to what had been, or so it seemed to him, a life spent in another dimension.

In that former life, the Larry Wortle he had then been could be genuinely, even if only faintly, amused, by a schoolgirl's, even a schoolmistress's, foolish letter. That other Larry had found himself quite interested, too, in the design which had just been submitted by Cartier for the setting of some magnificent Brazilian diamonds which had belonged to Lizzie's great-grandmother, and which had been shown at the Exhibition of '51.

But the Larry of those days had been transformed, as by a wave of Merlin's wand, into a passionate, exalted, entity, – always waiting, always watching, always above all longing, with a mingling of tender emotion and of brutal desire, for Cressida.

When Cressida was not there in the flesh to absorb his every thought, he spent the only time that mattered in living again through the bliss, which had been akin to anguish, of their last furtive meeting; aching for the rapt moment of ecstasy when his beloved would be once more in his arms, yielding him, with a reluctance which was half sincere, even when followed by a sudden superb abandonment, her lips.

Cressida had almost always shrunk from the manifestations of burning, authentic passion, much as she delighted in arousing passion in any man who, for a fleeting moment, attracted her. But in Larry Wortle she had found, to her own surprise, her complement. When they had first met, within a few moments of her arrival, each had experienced an incommunicable sensation, part physical, part mental, which had been at once a foretaste and a warning of all that had happened since.

But, unlike bemused Larry, Cressida knew, by now, that the pace was quickening dangerously, and she had made up her mind to "cut and run."

Oh, not for ever! She had no intention of giving up Larry Wortle. On the contrary, most definitely she intended to keep him her bounden slave for always. "Always" is a long time. But Cressida had seen, with a touch of envious interest, more than one such secret love endure till nothing remained, to the woman so blessed, of youth, beauty, and happiness – apart from that hidden tie. She had, however, decided to postpone any further friendship between Larry Wortle and herself till both he and she, especially he, were safely married.

After all, they would not have very long to wait.

Larry knew nothing of the plans for his future happiness already so intelligently thought out, and so positively decided on, in Cressida's mind. The one thought which filled his brain;

the only thing that mattered to him, now, was the fact that Cressida was going away the day after tomorrow, and that he must invent some scheme which would enable him to follow her at once – at once.

As to his relation to Lizzie Bowden, he still felt, and he was conscious of still feeling, for her while they sat, as they were sitting now, side by side, all that had ever been in his power to give, in exchange for all that her passionate love was about to bestow on him.

There even lay dormant, in the heart which now belonged so entirely to another, gratitude for her generous gift. Aye, and even gratitude for the further benefits which he knew were to be conferred on him in the future. But he was far past any possible feeling of shame or of remorse, and he believed his relation with his betrothed to be quite unimpaired.

And Lizzie? Lizzie, clad in a heavily-beaded salmon-pink frock which, to her aunt's anxious eyes, seemed to bring out to a special degree each of her worst physical points, had almost forgotten what had happened, during the few minutes she had been in the blue room early this afternoon. She was still too deeply absorbed in her own acute, jealous misery, to think of anything but Larry – Larry and the beautiful creature, now sitting just opposite to him, who had him in thrall.

***

After the three ladies had left the dining room, Cressida, feeling more pleasantly alive than she had felt for months, made Lady Bignor again laugh aloud, this time by her account of how a well-known woman had disguised herself as a Babu, and had taken in, at a great ball, the Secretary of State for India.

But just before the two men were due to come in from the dining room, the amusing teller of tales exclaimed: "I think I'll go upstairs now, Aunt Alice. I'm fearfully tired. May I stay in bed tomorrow morning, and skip church?"

Lady Bignor hesitated.

"I'm old-fashioned enough to feel that everybody ought to go to church on Christmas Day. Surely, my dear, you'll sleep extra well after motoring all those hours?"

"I should have slept – if I had lain down for a minute, after I came in. I was fearfully tempted by the sight of my delicious four-poster. However, I resisted the temptation."

"If you feel too tired to get up, you may stay in bed tomorrow morning. But in that case—" Lady Bignor shook a warning finger, "you'll have to submit to being treated as an invalid."

There had come to her a sudden perception that it would be a very good thing for everybody, including the naughty one herself, if Cressida stayed the whole of Christmas Day in bed.

But, "I'd hate to do that!" cried Cressida.

"I'll have the last dose of my best sleeping-stuff tonight! I've been saving it up, as I stupidly forgot to bring a fresh bottle, so I probably will get up tomorrow morning and go to church like a good girl."

Lizzie felt a curious, to her a hitherto unknown, sensation, composed half of mortal terror and half of fierce, ardent hope, steal into her burdened heart, as she heard the lightly uttered words, "I'll have the last dose of my best sleeping-stuff tonight!"

Cressida kissed her hostess goodnight with real warmth. In so far as she could love any woman, she did love Alice Bignor.

Then, from the door, "Ta-ta!" she called out. "And a happy Christmas to everybody; especially to you, little bride—"

As she disappeared softly, always Cressida Daryl performed with graceful deliberation all the little courtesies of life, Lady Bignor exclaimed, "She certainly is most amusing! I don't won-der she's so—" and then her voice died away.

She had caught a glimpse of Lizzie's ravaged face and, with startled surprise, saw the look of hatred in the desolate eyes which were still fixed on the door through which Cressida had just passed. Then the girl had not been really blind? Or, if she had been blind, her eyes were now opened. But what could have made Lizzie become so suddenly aware of her lover's treachery?

Then Lizzie's aunt remembered the motor drive which, beginning soon after lunch today, had only ended at half-past seven.

Why, those two young fools had been out for nearly five hours! It was that prolonged expedition – of course it was – which had awakened poor silly little Lizzie, at long last, to Larry's infatuation. It often takes such a small, apparently insignificant, occurrence, to start a train of right reasoning, even in a slow mind.

It was fortunate indeed that Cressida was leaving the day after tomorrow. Cressida's hostess threw a grateful thought to Lord Danesborough. Though he would never know it, he had done them all a very good turn.

This afternoon Lady Bignor had felt seriously annoyed with her amusing guest, as well as extremely angry with Larry Wortle. But by now her anger with one of the two sinners had evaporated. How dull tonight's dinner would have been without that Undine-like creature!

But Cressida's indulgent friend felt no softening as to Cressida's victim. Unpleasant and tiresome as would be the breaking-off of the engagement, she had now come to hope that the marriage would not take place. Being the manner of woman she was, however, she naturally wished to avoid anything that would look like an *esclandre* – and the look on Lizzie's pale set face had alarmed Lizzie's aunt, and made her hope, more than ever, that Cressida, after all, would stay in bed all day tomorrow.

10

LIZZIE BOWDEN AWOKE FROM a deep, though not from an untroubled, sleep, to see that her luminous clock marked three in the morning.

She had had such a curious dream – a dream unlike any she had ever had before, and she was given to dreams, aye, and to nightmares.

Her dream had been full of a queer, motiveless scurry and hurry, cut across, now and again, by strange horrible sounds, such as might have been emitted by some poor animal in pain.

She sat up in her bed, and a sensation of mortal terror began slowly, inexorably, to fold her round.

The house was astir – not a doubt of it! She could hear footsteps coming and going along the corridor outside her room, and up and down the back stairs.

Also doors were opening and shutting.

From far away droned the wheezy purr of a motor. Could it be? – yes, it was – Dr. McLeod's old heavy car.

Shivering with cold and fear, she jumped out of bed and saw, with a sensation of shrinking fear, a line of bright light under her bedroom door. Why should all the electric lights have been turned on in the corridor at this time of the night – or was it morning – Christmas morning?

She ran across to her door, and then she knelt down, and leant her quaking young body against it.

What was it that had happened, or was happening? Oh, if only she could hear what was going on the other side of the door.

Lizzie Bowden had often heard the expression, "listening at the keyhole;" and, in so far as she had thought of it at all, it had seemed to her a ridiculous, as well as of course a very dishonourable, thing to do. But now she took the key out of the lock of her door, and tried to see, as well as to hear, through the tiny aperture.

What an unexpected, and to her terrifying, sight appeared through that minute peephole!

In the centre of the brightly-lit corridor stood Colonel Slade, clad in a dark brown check dressing gown. He looked very grave, nay more than grave – distressed, and inexpressibly shocked. Lizzie could see his face gone white and drawn under the healthy tan.

All at once, Dr. McLeod came out of the blue room and, slowly, he closed the door behind him. He, too, looked grave and sad. But there was not on his face the expression of frozen horror that there was on the other man's face.

As the two met, they began talking together; and Lizzie wondered, with a feeling of extreme unease, what it was they were saying. She could only hear a murmured hum, hum, hum, for they were standing close to one another.

At last, feeling she could bear the suspense no longer, she rose from her knees, and opened her door very, very gently, just an inch or so. And at once, with startling clearness, she heard every word that was being uttered, or, rather, every word which came from Dr. McLeod's lips; for Colonel Slade stood silently listening to what the other man was saying, and there was on his familiar face still that awful look of stark horror.

"Thank God, there's no mystery about this tragedy – God knows it is a tragedy! But I have no doubt at all as to what happened, Colonel Slade. Indeed, it is so clear a case of accident that the possibility of suicide need not even be raised at the inquest."

Did the man he was addressing mutter, "I'm glad of that?" Lizzie thought he did.

Be that as it may, the other went on, "Miss Daryl was far too intelligent a young woman to choose such a painful method of death, had she even thought of doing away with herself, which she obviously had no idea of doing. It's a criminal thing to allow any form of liquid poison to go out in an ordinary bottle. I've always advocated the use of specially shaped bottles—"

Then Colonel Slade said something, but in so low a voice that Lizzie lost it. But she heard the quick answer, uttered in a tired, irritable voice,

"People do do strange things, when they're half asleep. And when they're wide awake, too, for the matter of that. My own wife was very nearly killed by just that sort of mistake made by a fully-trained nurse twenty years ago. It was within a fortnight of our first child's birth; and in broad daylight the monthly nurse actually poured out a big dose of poison in place of some harmless mixture."

The doctor paused, then he added sadly, "I'm very sorry for Lady Bignor. She was so fond of that poor girl. What a terrible Christmas Day this will mean for them all!"

And then Lizzie heard the man she always thought of as "Uncle George" say in a dull voice, "Terrible indeed."

Dr. McLeod exclaimed, and the eavesdropper wondered at the matter of fact way in which he spoke,

"I must be going now. There's nothing more that I can do. Will you kindly tell Lady Bignor that I'll see a note is sent to the coroner?

By the way, I'm afraid the police should be informed at once. They're apt to make themselves unpleasant if there's even the appearance of delay. So I'll see to that too."

The police?

Lizzie Bowden's lips opened, and emitted, without her being able to help it, a low, stuffless moan of abject terror.

The old doctor was slightly hard of hearing, but Colonel Slade turned sharply round, and Lizzie, in the eyes he fixed on the chink in her bedroom door, read, perhaps erroneously, a startled warning.

Though she knew that he could not see her, she shrank back in the darkness, every nerve taut, listening.

But Dr. McLeod had said all he had to say, and he began walking down the brightly-lit corridor, towards the staircase.

Colonel Slade remained standing in the same spot, just outside the blue room, and still gazed – was it anxiously, warningly? – at Lizzie's partly open door.

Then all at once he called out, "Why, here is Lady Bignor!" And slowly, a thought reluctantly, Dr. McLeod turned and came down the corridor again.

Lady Bignor had just emerged from the swing door which led from the back stairs. Tears were streaming down her face, and as she and the doctor met, Lizzie heard the quick interchange of whispered words: "Come now, you must try and pull yourself together, my dear friend," and she saw Dr. McLeod take up her aunt's hand, and pat it. "Those whom the gods love die young," he went on; "there's a lot of truth in that, you know?" And the broken sobbing reply, "Yes, I do know that."

A sudden sensation of bitter, hopeless repentance – repentance, not remorse – flooded Lizzie Bowden's oppressed heart.

But the most insistent of all human instincts, self-preservation, soon absorbed within itself every sentient element of her being. And it was with immeasurable relief that she overheard the consoling words, "It's such a blessing – you must let it be a real comfort to you – that it was so obviously an accident. Often, in such a case, there does remain a touch of painful doubt. But in this case there need be no shadow of doubt."

"I know that," sobbed Lady Bignor again. "But in a way that makes it all the more piteous! The poor darling was so happy,

Dr. McLeod. Such a nice man, a rich man too, has been longing to marry her for a long time; and at last she had made up her mind to say 'yes.' She told me so only yesterday. I – I think I shall have to write to him." Then, more calmly, she murmured: "You must go home now, at once. I know how fearfully tired you must be."

When Lizzie heard the two men's footsteps on the stairs leading down to the hall, she timorously opened her door wide.

"Aunt Alice! What is the matter?" she called out, in a voice she tried to make sound dazed and sleepy. "Is anybody ill? I thought I heard Dr. McLeod's voice just now."

Lady Bignor had always been an emotional woman, and now she ran, with a sudden cry, into her niece's dark bedroom, and took the girl into her arms.

Clutching her convulsively, and again bursting into tears, "Lizzie—" she cried, "Oh, Lizzie, a frightful thing has happened! Cressida – poor, poor Cressida is dead. She took a dose of poison, pure strychnine, by mistake last night – I suppose after she was in bed, about midnight, just before she turned out her light. And then, when she began to feel queer, she came and called me—"

Lizzie made an inarticulate sound. She felt as if she was being stifled, by those strong, clinging arms.

But her aunt only clutched her the closer. The mere feel of the warm young living body brought with it a vague feeling of comfort.

She went on, woefully, "It was terrible – terrible! Every moment of this awful night will haunt me to the day of my death. Though the doctor says it's perfectly clear that it was an accident, and though of course I'm sure it was an accident, it does seem so inexplicable – at any rate to me. Cressida was so clever, so quick – not at all the sort of person to make a mistake between a large bottle and a small bottle."

"I don't understand," faltered Lizzie, at last disengaging herself from her aunt's arms. She was trembling violently, her teeth chattering, possessed by that terrifying sensation which accompanies any sudden loss of self-control.

But Lady Bignor was far too absorbed in her own sensations of horror and of grief to notice anything strange in her niece's way of receiving the dreadful news. And she answered with a touch of impatience, and moving a little away from the girl as she did so,

"Yet what I've just told you is clear enough, my dear. There, on the toilet table in the blue room, are still the two bottles side by side. Dr. McLeod said we mustn't touch them till the police have seen them—"

Again that word of dread. Why should the police have to see the bottles? Lizzie dared not ask.

Her aunt went on in a lowered tone, "The larger bottle is empty. Cleary had noticed that there was just one dose left in it last evening, while she was waving Cressida's hair, before dinner. The glass stopper of the other, smaller, bottle, is loose. That, the doctor says, proves beyond doubt what happened. Cressida thought she was shaking out two or three drops of strychnine, instead of what was, in effect, a deadly dose. She had bought the stuff in Paris, and this was, unhappily, a very strong solution."

"I see what you mean, Aunt Alice—" muttered Lizzie.

She was still trembling, still feeling as if she could not govern the movements of her body; but, even so, she was making a violent effort to regain control over herself.

Lady Bignor put her hand over her eyes, as if to shut out a dreadful sight.

"It was frightful – frightful! It's extraordinary that you heard nothing. But Larry evidently heard nothing either. Of course he's not sleeping on this side of the house. I had to call Cleary and George Slade, and thank God, George Slade was able to get the dear old doctor as soon as was humanly possible. He had been out to a case, so he was able to come at once – at once. He was angelically kind – so quick and clever. But nothing could have saved her; all he could do was to deaden the pain a little."

Tears rose to her weary eyes, and ran down her face as she went on speaking, this time as if to herself.

"Cressida dead? Even now I can't believe it! Though the poor darling was always delicate, she was so full of vitality, so intensely alive—"

Lizzie said in a shaky voice, "You were awfully kind to her, Aunt Alice."

"I tried to be, God knows! And it was very nice of you, in the old days, never to be jealous of her, my dear. I'm afraid she wasn't always as kind to you as she might have been."

And then Lizzie said something which touched Lady Bignor, – touched and, even now, in her excited, agitated state, rather surprised her. Indeed, after they had been married and settled happily down together for what seemed quite a long time, when recalling, as sometimes she could not help doing, the events of this terrible night, Lizzie's aunt never told, even to her kind understanding George, what Lizzie now asked her aunt to do.

"Will you tell Larry, Aunt Alice? I – I'm afraid he will be very much upset."

"Of course I'll tell him, my dear! He's sure to be dreadfully distressed, as he and Cressida had become such friends."

She waited a moment, eager to get away from the images Lizzie's words, and her own words, had conjured up.

"George Slade is heartbroken. He told Dr. McLeod he'd never seen anything so horrible – even in the war. But oh, he was such a comfort to me! Such a comfort even to that poor tortured girl, before the doctor arrived."

***

It was a strange sunny Christmas morning in the hushed house of death.

As for Lizzie – after a red-eyed housemaid, instead of her own maid, who, it seemed, had also been up most of the night, had brought her a cup of tea – she got up, taking as long as she could over her bath and her dressing.

Then, forgetting for the first time in her life that there was such a thing as breakfast in the world, she went straight down to the study, and sat there, feeling cold and sick with fear, by a fire she had had to light herself.

About nine o'clock there came sounds of a heavy car being driven quickly up through the grounds of Millhanger House; and the front-door bell pealed insistently.

Lizzie leapt out of her chair. That must be – that was, the police from Guildford.

She heard the tramp of men's booted feet going up the staircase; and, after what seemed to her a long time, though it was only a very few minutes, she heard them coming down again.

And then, from the hall which was only separated from the study by a small lobby, came the murmur of unfamiliar masculine voices, and, to Lizzie's excited imagination, it was as if, now and again, her own name, Elizabeth Bowden, emerged from that low-pitched babel of human sound.

Was everyone in the house going to be questioned and cross-questioned as to what they had done yesterday?

There darted into her terror-haunted mind a scene in a play to which she had once been taken. It showed a woman, a girl, being subjected to what someone had told her was called "the third degree" – she couldn't think why.

Were they going to do that to her in a few minutes? If so, she must be ready for their questioning.

She stared fearfully at the closed door of the study, and suddenly she gave an involuntary cry, for the door seemed to be opening slowly, slowly.

Then, gradually, she realised that the door had not moved at all. It was still shut – shut as it had been by herself, an hour ago. It was her nerves, her conscience, which had played her that terrifying trick.

Still quivering with fear she sat down again by the fire, and held out her hands to the now leaping flames.

Surely Aunt Alice would protect her from stupid, frightening, useless questions? Why, she knew nothing – nothing that would help the police.

If George Slade, who always told the truth, revealed how he had seen her leaving the blue room at lunch time, she must of course admit that she had gone in there.

But – but she could explain that she had had an excellent reason for doing so. She had wanted to find a scarf Cressida had offered to lend her. They had all heard Cressida offer to lend her that scarf, the last time she had gone out with Larry in his two-seater.

True, she had rejected the kind offer, but, yesterday afternoon, she had changed her mind and thought she would like to have it.

Unluckily she had not been able to find the scarf. That was why it hadn't been in her hand when she had met Colonel Slade just outside the blue room . . .

She lost count of time as she went over and over again her lying story. Fear held her – dreadful, agonising, fear.

But all at once she staggered to her feet, and a wild look of hope and of suspense filled her white face.

She had heard the front door open, and a moment later she saw the top of the police car flash past above the evergreen bushes which hid the road beyond the wide lawn.

Sinking down again into the low chair, she closed her eyes, infinitely thankful for what might be, after all, only a respite. . .

It might have been an hour later, or only a few minutes, when the door of the study opened – really opened this time. And then, looking round, Lizzie saw Larry Wortle advancing, with dragging feet, towards her.

She tried to get up. But it was as if her body refused to obey her brain. So she remained huddled up in the deep chair by the fire.

When he was close to her Larry knelt down, and taking hold of her hands, "Darling," he muttered brokenly, "Lady Bignor has just told me of the awful, awful thing which happened last night—"

She could hardly hear the whispered words, but she squeezed his fingers convulsively.

"Somehow I can't believe it," he went on in stifled tones. "She was such a wonderful creature! So full of vitality and life—"

He looked up, and his ravaged face was unconsciously asking for her help, almost for her sympathy.

But what he said was, "She always spoke of you so awfully nicely, Lizzie."

The girl made a restless movement, and he blundered on, speaking his thoughts aloud. No conscious hypocrite, yet, in a sense, marking time, and feeling, even in the midst of his frightful sense of loss, a measure of relief, as Lizzie – her great love for him giving her a sixth sense – dimly apprehended.

"She was so looking forward to going with us to Egypt, darling! She had a lot of friends there; it would have been such fun."

"Such fun?" Larry Wortle's vocabulary was limited.

"I wish I could be of some use to Lady Bignor," he exclaimed, trying hard, as even she realised, to pull himself together. "But Colonel Slade and the doctor are seeing to everything. There seems nothing I can do. And – and darling?"

"Yes?" whispered Lizzie.

It was the first time since Larry had come into the room that she had opened her lips.

"Lady Bignor thinks it would be better for us two to go away this morning – up to London. She's already telephoned and arranged with your godmother to put us both up for a few days."

A sensation of intense, exultant, joy flooded Lizzie Bowden's whole being.

She leant forward and threw her arms round the man she now felt again to be hers – all hers.

"I think that's a very good idea," she murmured.

Then she laid her cheek against his.

"I'm afraid you must be feeling very upset, Larry," she whispered, in a feeling tone. "You and poor Cressida had become such friends – hadn't you?"

"Yes, we had, in a way," he answered in a muffled voice.

Then Lizzie had suspected nothing? Consciously he thanked God for that. What a brute he had been – what a cad – to this poor little girl who cared for him so much!

There came over him a feeling of abject shame, as he remembered yesterday, and the day before yesterday, and the day before that.

At last he raised his head, and, for the first time, as far as he, Larry Wortle, was concerned, their lips met in a lovers' kiss.

THE END

Q.E.D.
by Lynn Brock

There's Death in the Churchyard
by William Gore

Murder of the Ninth Baronet
by J.S. Fletcher

Dead Man Manor
by Valentine Williams

The Man in the Dark
by John Ferguson

The Dressing Room Murder
by J.S. Fletcher

Glory Adair and the Twenty-First Burr
by Victor Lauriston

The Tunnel Mystery
by J.C. Lenehan

Murder on the Marsh
by John Ferguson

The Fatal Five Minutes
R.A.J. Walling

The Crime of a Christmas Toy
Henry Herman

Death of an Editor
Vernon Loder

Death on May Morning
Max Dalman

The Hymn Tune Mystery
George A. Birmingham

The Middle of Things
JS Fletcher

The Essex Murders
Vernon Loder

The Boat Race Murder
R. E. Swartwout

Who Killed Alfred Snowe?
J. S. Fletcher

Murder at the College
Victor L. Whitechurch

*The Yorkshire
Moorland Mystery*
J. S. Fletcher

Fatality in Fleet Street
Christopher St. John Sprigg

The Doctor of Pimlico
William Le Queux

The Charing Cross Mystery
J. S. Fletcher

Fatality in Fleet Street ePub & PDF
FREE when you sign up for our
infrequent Newsletter.